Life, Love, and Other Inequalities

Argentina Ryder

I0587988

Contessina Publishing

Copyright

For C

Contents

August

To: All_Staff_HaysMS
From: Curtis White
Date: August 14
Subject: First week of school agenda

Welcome back, Hays Hawks, to the new school year! Please plan to meet bright and early on Monday August 21st at 8 AM in the cafeteria. PTA is providing breakfast tacos and coffee.

There have been couple of changes since we last met together as a group that you will notice when you return:

* Jon Levy has taken a position at Granger High School as their choir teacher.

* Gina Jimenez and her family have moved to California for family reasons.

We wish them well on their future adventures. We also wish to congratulate Dorothy Lopez on the birth of her daughter, Alexis. Mother and daughter are doing well, and we will see Mrs. Lopez back on campus later this fall. Please review the attached draft for the required meetings for the rest of the week. See you soon!

— — —

Curtis White
Principal, Sarah Hays Middle School

· · · · ●●· ●· · ·

E stella, Texas, population 22,000, sat conveniently east of San Antonio, west of Houston, and south of Austin. Residents had access to resources afforded to the bigger cities when they required it, like medical care and higher education, but Estella still kept that small-town feeling that its citizens enjoyed. It boasted an outdoor mall with a couple of anchor stores, two grocery chains, and a retail shopping center with most of the big box stores represented. One high school, two middle schools, and a handful of elementary schools made up the school district. But for Matt Ruiz, the most exciting addition in recent memory was the twenty-four-hour gym that opened close to his house this past summer.

Matt arrived at the gym promptly at six. The franchise was owned by a teacher out of San Antonio who offered generous discounts to others in the profession, so he recognized several of the regulars from various district department trainings or from athletics. Matt jumped onto a treadmill and inserted his ear buds, adjusting the volume of his music to something that wouldn't break his eardrums.

As he jogged, he went over a quick rundown of his day: gym, quick shower, stop for coffee, be at school by eight AM for the faculty meeting, then work in his classroom. He packed a sack lunch (ham and cheese with pickles on white) but if history served him right, someone would suggest a group lunch at Gringo's celebrating—or lamenting—their return to work. Matt would get the enchilada plate; it was always an excellent choice and usually the lunch special on Mondays. Home by five, work on a discussion post for his graduate class, check in on his grandparents, and get everything ready that he needed for Tuesday. In bed by eleven.

A busy day, but those were the best.

Matt caught a glimpse of himself in the gym mirrors. Not too bad, he decided. Five foot eleven—not the tallest guy in the room, but fit and trim. Black hair cropped short, dark eyes rimmed by thick black lashes, and a smile described as charming when he felt so inclined. "*Que chulo*," his grandma would tell him, her hand on his cheek. *How cute.* She wouldn't lie, right?

Two miles later, he sat down on the rowing machine, adjusted the tension, and started his workout. His phone vibrated just as the rowing machine's twenty-minute alarm chimed.

It was Cora. *Going to Starbucks this morning, what do you want?*

Bless that angel. Matt responded with his usual order and headed for the shower, checking the clock on his phone. 6:45 AM. Right on time.

· · · ● · ● · · · ·

Pulling into the parking lot of Hays Middle School an hour later, Matt recognized several familiar faces parking in alongside him, all the teachers returning to school after their time away. They waved at each other, friends and coworkers, as everyone made toward the cafeteria for their annual first-week-back faculty meeting. Matt slung his backpack over his shoulder and walked inside. Every few feet, someone stopped him to say hello and ask what Matt had been up to over the summer break. Laverne, who taught history, pulled out her phone and showed him pictures of her holiday at the Grand Canyon, while Stella, who taught science, was already complaining about complications with the schedule.

Eventually Matt made it to the cafeteria, searching for the other math teachers and spotting them bunched up on the left side of the room. Once he found his table, Matt dropped his backpack and settled into an uncomfortable plastic chair across from his department head. "How long is Dorothy's maternity leave?" Matt asked, straight to the point.

"And it's delightful to see you too, Mr. Ruiz," Deanna retorted, digging into her vibrant, oversized tote bag, the bright red bag nearly the same shade as her hair. She sighed, pulling out a yellow highlighter and a ballpoint pen. "I'm not sure. Last I heard, it was at least a month."

"Shit," Matt murmured. Starting off the year without a proper math teacher could set the kids up for failure.

Just as he opened his mouth to speak, a large paper coffee cup appeared in front of him. "Venti Americano with almond milk and two Stevias."

Yes. "*Gracias*, Cora," he said to the young woman who sat next to him, her dark skin set off by her bright smile and white shirt.

"*De nada*, Matt. Good morning, Mrs. Bush." Cora gave her an approving nod. "Nice tan. You go to the coast this summer?"

"Welcome back, Cora." Deanna laughed, looking down at her arms. "Alas, just stayed home and took the kids to the neighborhood pool." Tilting her head, she leaned in closer to Cora. "Any news from Dorothy?" Cora was the special education teacher assigned to work with the math department. She and Dorothy had worked together for the past two years, and the women were close friends.

Cora Mann's smile fell as she carefully took the lid off her coffee, blowing across the top. "I have, and it's not good news." Cora shook her head, looking at each of them. "November. That's what I was told."

Deanna and Matt's faces both froze. "November?" Matt repeated. "But that's—"

"Ten weeks." Cora gave a little snort. "She says she can afford it. Any idea what they've got planned? Lopez teaches the classes with the special ed kids. This is more than being a substitute for a day or two," she added. "A long-term sub needs to teach, not just stand there and hand out worksheets." She sighed, stirring her coffee. "I think they scheduled my kids in there the first part of the day."

Before Deanna could respond, more teachers arrived and joined them at the table. The staff usually arranged themselves by department, with the newbies who clung to each other at the back table after spending the previous week together at new teacher training.

The chatter grew louder as more people arrived. They exchanged greetings and welcome backs, while they ate their breakfast tacos and bad coffee. Matt spotted Rebecca Hogan, their vice principal, dimming the lights for their slide show presentation, and soon their administrative team all made their way to the front of their cafetorium, debating on whether to use the microphone.

New year, same shit, Matt thought to himself as their principal formally greeted the staff.

"Welcome back, Hays Hawks," Curtis White called out to the smattering of sleepy applause. His dark brown goatee had more gray in it this year, giving him even more of an intimidating look.

"Yes, I realize it's early, but I can speak for all of us up here that we're glad to have everyone back."

Deanna was texting wildly on her phone. As head of the math department, Deanna Bush was responsible for making certain Dorothy's sub was in place and ready to go next week. Department head was a thankless job, and while the consensus was that Matt was next in line if Deanna ever left, right now he thanked all the gods that he didn't have those worries this year.

As it was, he had too much on his plate already.

"Matt." Someone was calling his name, waving a stack of papers in his hand.

Matt reached out and grabbed the handouts, taking one and passing the others down. This was the important info: last year's test scores, various extracurricular duties, and most important—lunch times. Pulling out his highlighter from his own backpack, he began noting anywhere he saw his name and marking it bright yellow.

"We don't eat together this year." Cora's face fell as she rifled through her handouts. "I'm at eleven, and you're at eleven-thirty."

"It was good while it lasted," Matt replied, reading over the papers. "But you'll find another sucker to borrow change from for the soda machine." He feigned pain when she punched his arm.

He continued going through his forms, moving ahead of the official presentation. Test scores were good last year; his classes did excellent. His after-school duty assignment was... helping get kids on the busses. *Shit*, he thought as he highlighted his name and turned the page, the meeting droning on.

The morning progressed the same as it had the last five years Matt had taught here at this school. He remembered that day when he'd first arrived at Sarah Hays Middle School and had sat at the newbie table. Teachers had and gone, table positions had changed, but the information the administrators presented seemed the same every year. The principal introduced new staff, the vice principal talked about the mission statement, and the assistant principal pushed the PTA T-shirt sales.

Matt's phone vibrated. Half past nine, and the group chat was already discussing lunch ideas. He was about to answer when he felt a hand on his shoulder. Looking up, he blinked, surprised to see their principal, who'd left the others at the front and had wandered over to their table.

"Matt, come talk to me when you have a minute, after the meeting's over."

"Yes, sir." Matt watched as Curtis strode back to the front of the cafeteria to dismiss the staff from the morning meeting. Curious. He glanced over at Deanna. "You know what that's about?" he asked, worried, as he gathered his scattered papers.

She shook her head. "No idea. Go talk to him, and come by my room when you're done if you need to vent." To the table, she called out, "Math department, my room at two this afternoon. Bring your calendars."

· · · • •• • • • · ·

"Good morning, Rosa."

"Hey there, Matt. How was your summer?" Rosa Mendez, the principal's secretary, always wore vivid colors, and today was no exception. Her bright yellow dress brightened up the otherwise drab front office at the school.

"It was good, ma'am. Curtis said to come by and chat with him. Is he in there?" Matt pointed down the hall.

"Yes, he mentioned he was expecting you." She gestured toward his office. "I think he's alone right now. You'd better hurry before someone else jumps in there. Busy day, you know."

"Mr. Ruiz. Glad to have you back."

Matt stepped into Curtis White's office, Dallas Cowboys memorabilia hanging alongside framed diplomas from TCU and UTSA. "Hello, Mr. White." Matt closed the door behind him and took the seat across from the principal's desk, folding his hands in front of him, feeling a little like a chastened student. "I hope you had a pleasant summer."

"Likewise," Curtis replied. "I got your email over the summer about your graduate school classes. Tell me what that's about."

Matt smiled broadly, proud of this undertaking. "I'm working toward a Master's degree in Educational Leadership. Most of the classes online are taught online, but I might have to run into town for tests and meetings with the professors."

"Outstanding," Curtis replied with his own matching smile. "What are your end plans? What is the target we're going for?"

"District leadership," Matt answered without hesitation. "I enjoy the classroom, but I think I can make a difference in a district position. Ultimately, I want to be a superintendent one day. Maybe not this district—" he smiled, "—but somewhere."

Curtis raised an eyebrow. "That doesn't surprise me at all. You'll be great at that, and with your work ethic, I have no doubt you'll succeed. Just let me know what we can do to help you out, if you need to shadow any of us for the day, or come by and pick our brains for an assignment."

Matt grinned, thankful for the encouragement. "I appreciate that," he said to the older man. "I understand it's a lot, taking on this master's degree program along with the algebra class and helping with the athletics department." The year hadn't started, but Matt could anticipate all that needed to be done. "But I'm ready for the challenge, and I don't expect things to get easier next year, so I thought, what am I waiting for?" According to Matt's master plan (and the accompanying spreadsheet) for his career, he was right on time.

Curtis White's face fell somewhat. "That makes this much harder to ask. I have a special project for you, for a few weeks. You're aware Dorothy's out for a couple of months?"

Shit. Matt took a deep breath, bracing his features. "Until first week of November, that's what I was told."

"Sounds about right." Glancing down at his desk, Curtis picked up a yellow Post-it note with scribbling on it. "I'd like your help with our long-term substitute. He's brand new to the school and the district, so he might need someone to show him the lay of the land, maybe help with the lesson plans and all that. His name's—" Curtis looked down at the paper, "—Sawyer Evans." He passed the note to Matt, who reached out and accepted it. "He'll attend all math department meetings, so he should pick up the curriculum pretty quick."

"Certified?" Matt asked hopefully.

"No, but a college graduate. Pretty sure." Curtis wrinkled in thought. "I'll check on that for you."

Shit. Matt drew a deep breath. "Curtis—"

But Curtis didn't let him finish. "I understand. This isn't an ideal situation for anyone. But Ms. Mann will work in the classroom with Mr. Evans throughout the day, and while her priority is helping the special ed students, we're hoping she helps guide him with the classroom management. Show him how to work with the kids, especially the ones in the program. But he might need a teacher from the math department assisting him with the curriculum. Deanna's got a lot on her plate this year too, so we're asking you can do this for us." Curtis gave him a confident smile. "He'll be here first thing tomorrow. I think he's stuck in HR hell today."

"When you put it like that..." Matt said. "I'll find him tomorrow morning." But inwardly, he cursed. This was the absolute last thing he needed right now, a babysitting assignment for a newbie. But another voice in his head reminded him it never hurt to do a favor for the principal, someone who could give him a solid recommendation when it was his turn to work as an administrator.

Well, that was that. Curtis nodded at him, letting him know the meeting was over.

Matt stood, scratching his hair and grinning as he changed the subject. "I talked to Paul last night. He thinks the eighth-grade football team might go undefeated in district this year." Their smaller district often played the bigger schools from San Antonio, schools with more money and support, but as of late, they'd been holding their own.

"That group of boys had a hell of a year last fall. It's not inconceivable." Curtis stood, extending his hand. "Thanks again, Matt. Keep me in the loop with how he's doing, if you all need more help from us in any way."

· · · · ●· ●· · · ·

After saying goodbye to Rosa, Matt left the front office and walked down the hallway toward the gymnasium, lightly tapping the lockers hanging on the walls as he walked. In a week, the kids would swell the hallways, grades six through eight. Matt had hesitated at first when offered the job of teaching math at Hays Middle School, five years ago now. Teaching had never been his dream, but once he'd made that decision, changing his major from engineering to education, Matt had assumed he'd work at the high school, teaching higher math, inspiring the minds of aspiring engineers and scientists.

But it was the middle school that had had a job opening, and five years later, here he was. Time had flown by, and a wry smile crossed Matt's face as he thought about his students. Excitable, malleable, silly. It wasn't awful, he admitted to himself. And it wasn't forever. Matt had a timeline, and so far, everything was right on track.

Pushing open the heavy gym doors, Matt made a right turn toward the boys' locker rooms. He spotted the coaches near the equipment cages, separating football uniforms into different sizes. "Hey."

"Matt." Paul Cross waved him over. Tall and broad, his thin, gray hair was even sparser than it had been at the conclusion of the previous school year. "What's the good word? Clint here said Curtis called you in for a talk."

Matt nodded, reaching over and helping them sort. "Yeah, I've got some extra duties this year. For a couple of months, anyway."

"That's a fucking shame." Paul chuckled as he handed Clint a couple of pairs of pants. "At least you aren't in trouble or anything. Hey, we're going over to Buddy's for lunch if you wanna join us."

Matt smiled to himself. It hadn't been easy back when Matt had first been hired. He'd grown up in and around Estella, so people around town knew he was gay. But he was discreet and a hard worker, and those disapproving coworkers could ignore his sexual orientation if they wanted. Matt certainly didn't care. Then the opportunity had come to work with the athletic department, and Matt had worried about finding his place among these guys, these "men's men," these cowboy coaches. Would they accept someone like him in their ranks?

But they'd given each other a chance, and now Matt counted them among his best friends here at the school. "Thanks, but I think I'm going with the math department today. We got a new guy on board for a couple of months. Curt said I'm helping him get settled and figure out what he needs to learn."

"Well, shit," Clint said in that "good ole boy" drawl of his, exaggerated for comedic effect. "Sorry to hear 'bout that."

"It is what it is." He looked around the coaches' office. "But I don't plan on neglecting the team. Every day, eighth period, I'll be here. Just let me know what you need from me, and I'll get it done."

It was after eleven before Matt made it upstairs to his own classroom. Standing in the doorway of the empty room, he thought back to his own first day of teaching. Five years now at this school. Back then he'd thought it was about teaching math, him standing in the front of the room, his students sitting at their desks absorbing his words. Now his expectations more in line with reality, but that didn't make it any less interesting. Matt wouldn't quite call it thrilling, but as he sat down at his computer and read over the lists of student names, some new and some familiar, he felt a pang of excitement at the idea of the new year and all that could happen.

Creating independent learners, strong thinkers, reliable citizens of the world, with the occasional two-step equation tossed in there for good measure.

Six of them ended up at Gringo's for lunch. "I don't understand why they hired someone brand new for a long-term sub job," Matt grumbled as the server set the enchilada plate in front of him, still pissed about his additional duty. "Why didn't they ask Margie to sub? She at least knows the school and how it all works."

Deanna snorted, digging into her taco salad. "They did. She turned them down. Same with Mr. Garza—he didn't want to be tied down. Ten weeks is a long time, and I guess no one wanted to commit to that."

"Seventh grade math, that's the worst too," Alicia added with a cheeky grin.

"You teach sixth grade reading." Alex made a face. "Literally the worst."

"Literally," Alicia answered, and Matt leaned back, chuckling as they started one of their familiar debates. It felt good to be back with friends.

•••••••••

That evening, Matt flipped off his computer after finishing his discussion post for his Schools and Community Relations class. He went to the kitchen to prepare his lunch when he remembered he hadn't eaten today's meal, and it was still at school in the teacher's lounge fridge. That task checked off his list, he pulled out his phone and called his grandmother.

"Hey there." Matt opened up his pantry, looking for a snack. "How was your day?" he asked, pulling out some peanut butter and crackers.

His grandmother launched into a tirade. "You need to come get your grandpa. Otherwise, I might kick him out of the house."

Matt smiled. It was a threat she made often, and always in jest. "What did he do now?"

"It's those damn four-wheelers that you and Sabrina bought. They're too fast for him, and I told him not to use them, but does he listen to me? No, and he's going to fall and break his neck one of these days."

"He's a stubborn old goat," Matt admitted, "but that's why you love him, right?"

She sighed. "I suppose. But I'm still worried about it."

"I'll talk to him and ask him to let Sabrina do those chores from now on. Or—" he looked up at the ceiling, "—maybe I can come out and help more often, if you need." Matt didn't have the time, but he'd find it somehow if they needed him.

That promise soothed her. "Thank you, *mijo*. Maybe he'll listen to you." She paused. "Ay, *Dios mío*, I didn't even ask you how your day was! Did you get to meet all your students?"

"It was okay. It's gonna be a good year. No, the kids aren't there yet. They get another week of summer break." They talked for a few more minutes, and after the call ended, Matt answered a few texts from friends, watched some television, and climbed into bed.

It had been a solid day, all things considered.

· · · · ● · ● · · · ·

Tuesday morning, Matt arrived on campus just after seven. He walked toward his room to work on setting things up when he noticed the door to C106 open, the light on and spilling over into the hallway. Most of the time, Matt was the first to arrive in his hallway and rarely did anyone beat him, so he walked over to see if the new substitute had arrived.

Taking a deep breath, Matt knocked on the frame of the open door. "Mr. Evans?" he asked, peering around the empty classroom, desks in neat, ordered rows.

"Over here!" a voice called out from behind the teacher's desk. Matt walked into the room, following the sound. "I'm just — Ow, hold on..." Matt sat on the edge of a student desk, waiting. "I can't—" Then a man appeared, head popping up like a prairie dog from under the teacher's desk, and Matt had to stifle a grin. "Heya," the other man said. "Sorry, I'm trying to get this computer hooked up to that monitor. Or to the projector, I'm not sure," he added, biting his lip, hands full of tangled black cords.

Unbelievable. "I can help you with that later. I'm Matt Ruiz. I teach two doors down."

The other man stood, taller than Matt, stretching to hold out his hand. He grinned, a bright smile lighting his entire face. His very attractive face. "Sawyer. Sawyer Evans, long-term sub." He had a light beard and a messy dark-blond top knot that made him appear even taller. The sleeves of his gray Henley were pushed up on his long arms, displaying colorful tattoos on both forearms. "I understand you're going to help me out over here. Thanks in advance."

Matt took his hand, shaking it. "Don't mention it. Do you have a minute to talk?" he asked curtly, noting the chaotic state of the room and teacher's desk. "No offense, but I've got a lot to do today."

"Oh yeah, of course." Sawyer stepped out behind the desk. "I just got here, and I'm already a week behind."

That wasn't far from the truth, Matt suspected. He pulled a student desk close to the teacher's desk and sat down, opening his binder. "This is a list of all the faculty meetings and other trainings we have scheduled this week," he said, handing the other man a sheet of paper. "The ones highlighted in yellow are the ones you need to attend. The ones in green would be helpful, but not mandatory." Sawyer's lips quirked, as if holding back a smile. Matt ignored it and continued. "On the back I wrote some important phone numbers and email addresses, if you need to get a hold of us. If you have questions, these are the people to call. It's always better to call than to get it wrong and have someone have to fix it for you later."

Sawyer exhaled slow. "Will do." He took the paper and reviewed it, flipping it back and forth.

"Have you met Cora?" Matt asked.

"Ms. Mann?" Sawyer shook his head. "Not yet. She texted me she'll be here around nine this morning to set up her desk in the back of the room and talk me through what the classes are like."

"She's your special ed component. You'll have all the students with academic disabilities. She's going to help you with their assignments." Sawyer's eyes grew wide for a minute. "I won't lie, it's an enormous responsibility, being the teacher with those students. But Cora's the best. Do whatever she says, and you'll be okay."

"She won't be here all the time, though, will she?"

Matt shook his head. "Three out of six classes." He pulled another set of papers out of his binder. "Here are your student lists in each class. Cora will tell you who needs extra help." He handed over another stack. "This is the district's math scope and sequence for the first quarter." Another stack. "These are the middle school math standards the kids should learn during your time here."

Sawyer accepted them all silently, and Matt wondered if he now regretted taking on this assignment.

Looking down at his watch, he noticed the time. "Cora will be a big help once she gets here. I'm right down the hall in C103. My cell number is on that list, along with my classroom phone number. Call if you have questions."

"I apologize in advance for how many times I'm going to call you." Sawyer looked up at him, bright blue eyes filled with a lot more worry than they had at the beginning of their conversation. "But I appreciate all the effort you've already put in. I'm going to try my best not to be too much of a burden."

Deanna Bush introduced Sawyer at the math department meeting on Tuesday. "Mr. Evans will take over for Mrs. Lopez's seventh graders for a couple of months while she's out on maternity leave. Matt Ruiz has agreed to help with anything Mr. Evans needs, but I know we'll all chip in when we can. Sawyer, please don't hesitate to ask anyone for help if you have a question or a problem. It's easier to fix problems before they get too serious, and all of us here want to help you as much as we can."

Sawyer looked over at Matt and grinned. "That's what I hear. I promise not to get into too much trouble."

That smile... Matt felt his face flush. He swallowed. *Don't you dare, Mateo Ruiz. No. Not here, not now.*

· · · · • · • · · ·

Friday morning brought another faculty meeting. Matt found himself across from Sawyer, who sat next to Cora, listening as she explained the game plan for Monday. "There's not much going on math-wise. It's mostly procedural—learning their names, filling out forms, passing out textbooks." Sawyer's face tried to hide how over his head he was, but Cora put her hand on his shoulder. "You'll be fine. Won't he be fine, Matt?" she asked, pulling him into the conversation.

"On Monday? Yeah, he'll be fine on Monday. Now Tuesday, that's another story." Matt opened his backpack and pulled out another colored folder. "Tuesday is when all hell breaks loose."

Cora glared. "You're not helping. What is that?"

"The rest of the week." Matt handed each of them a typed-out lesson plan with objectives and assignments listed for each day. "Alex gave this to me." Matt pointed at the older man sitting next to Deanna. "He teaches the other sections of seventh grade. He'll do the lesson plans and make the assignments while Dorothy's out. I printed out copies of the lessons so you'd both have a hard copy—Dorothy used to give you hard copies the week before, right, Cor?"

She nodded, her glare softening. "Yes, so I could start looking at ways to accommodate the assignments for some of our kids." Matt watched her point out a couple of problems to Sawyer, explaining how she would alter worksheets for her students. "Thanks, Matt."

"No problem. Alex will share the folder with you with all the digital files." Matt dropped another packet in front of Sawyer. "Here are the answer keys for next week's lessons."

Sawyer's eyes widened again. "You didn't have to do all of this," he said. "But thanks."

Matt grunted. "Yeah, I kinda did. We need to make certain you understand what's going on, lesson-wise. Look over the assignments. If something doesn't make sense, call one of us and we'll walk you through it." Looking between Cora and Sawyer, he added, "It'll be hard enough keeping the parents happy once they learn there's a substitute for two months. Can't have them thinking the sub can't teach."

"I won't let you down." Sawyer caught Matt's eye and held it for a long second. "I promise."

Matt held that gaze a second longer, unsure why, but he didn't want to be the first to break it. "You'll be fine." Just then, Curtis began speaking, and everyone turned their attention to the speakers standing in the front.

Everyone except Matt, who couldn't stop looking at Sawyer. Matt, momentarily mesmerized by a small scar on the side of the man's face, peeking out of that light stubble.

Matt, who now realized what kind of trouble he was in for this fall. *Shit.*

·········

On Monday morning, Matt was at the school bright and early per usual. He prided himself on being an early bird, but today a few others were early as well. Unexpected surprises always happened on the first day—computer malfunctions, nervous parents wandering around, jammed copy machines...sometimes all three. He sipped from his Hays Hawks coffee mug (a PTA fundraiser from the previous year) as he made his way down the hall of the C wing toward his room and spotted an open door with the light on.

The new guy was an early bird too, at least today. Matt glanced inside. "Hey." Sawyer and Cora had stocked the front table with supplies, textbooks lined up on the bookshelves, and Sawyer was hanging up a couple of posters in the back of the room. On one of them, a kitten and puppy leaned against each other in a garden setting with the words "Be a friend!" written in bright lettering on the bottom. "You ready for today?" Matt asked as he stepped into the room.

Sawyer turned toward his voice and smiled. He wore a crisp white button-down shirt with rolled-up sleeves and khakis, hair pulled back into a tidy bun. "Morning," he called out. "I guess I'd better be." A slightly panicked look crossed his face as he glanced around the empty room, absently stroking his chin hair. "They'll be here soon."

"That they will." Other teachers began making their way down the halls, waving at him and getting on with the business of starting the day. "I'd better go get ready," Matt said, reconciling himself to the fact that he was crushing on the new guy. "Good luck today. Call me if you need any help."

Several hours later, Matt packed his bag at the end of seventh period, once he'd collected all ice-breaker activities the class completed.

A boy in the front row raised his hand. "Are you coaching again this year, Mr. Ruiz?"

He nodded. "If you're in athletics, I'll meet you down in the gym next period." The bell rang, and a few kids stood and started for the door, sitting back down once they saw his frowning face. Once everyone settled back into their seats, Matt announced, "You're dismissed. See you tomorrow, class."

Just like that, his first day of teaching this year was over.

He saw Sawyer in the hallway, greeting students as they entered his classroom for their eighth period class. "How's it going?"

"I'm exhausted," Sawyer admitted, "and all we've done are ice breakers. But the day went quick. I can't believe it's almost over."

Matt snickered. "Well, the good news is you get to come back and do it again tomorrow."

· · • •· • • · · ·

The first week flew by, like it invariably did. Matt's morning classes went smoothly, but those were his algebra students, high-achieving kids working for high school credits. The classes after lunch were his eighth regular math students, many of them acting as if they were still on their summer sleep schedules. "I'm hoping the yawns and glassy stares I'm seeing are from fatigue because you retained all this information over the summer, and not because I'm boring you."

"I never learned any of this," one girl told him, a serious expression on her face as she stared at the paper. "None of it."

Matt stepped over to his desk and reached for the telephone. "I'm calling Mrs. Lopez right now and telling her you suggested she didn't spend a week teaching this last year."

Several students began chattering excitedly at the mention of their former teacher. "When is she coming back?" another student asked. "I want to say hi to her."

"Will she bring the baby to school when she comes back?"

"Her sub is super cute." Two girls began whispering about Sawyer. "I hope he stays for a long time."

Matt silently agreed, but only narrowed his eyes at the students. "Well, what I hope is that someone can explain calculating simple interest." Turning, he wrote on the white board in large capital letters. "I = PRT. What does the T stand for?" he asked again, and turned toward the class, his heart falling at all the blank stares he saw returned to him. Hopefully, it was just the first-week sleepies. "Alright, let's review."

It didn't take long for the other teachers to concur with him. "They're not even trying," Alicia stated emphatically, standing next to the microwave as she waited for her frozen burrito to heat. "All we were working on today was filling out this getting-to-know-you bullshit worksheet." When the microwave beeped, she took her dish out and walked over to the table. "How do you not know your favorite food?"

Cynthia took her place at the microwave, tearing the plastic film off her frozen lunch. "We started talking about family histories as a preface for our introduction to world cultures next week. I've already had two parent emails asking why I'm being, and I quote, 'so nosy' about their families. I'm not asking for skeletons in their closet, I just want you to know where your grandma came from."

Steve, the art teacher, sat down next to Matt. "Hey, how're you holding up? Been busy?" he asked as he took his grocery store salad out of his brown lunch bag.

"Not a minute to breathe." Matt pulled his sandwich out of his insulated bag. "I've got two preps, three if you count Lopez's kids, and athletics during eighth period. Also started grad school this summer," he told them. "I'm taking a couple of classes this fall."

The others all smiled and congratulated him. Cynthia clapped. "Not too much longer until you're Principal Ruiz," she said. "You'll remember us little people in the trenches when you're off in the land of giants, right?" Everyone laughed. "So, how's it going with Lopez's long-term guy?"

Matt nodded, chewing quickly. "So far, so good. Cora's with him the first part of the day, so that helps. She can go over the classroom management and any of the math she knows. But we can't ask her to design lessons and grade and fill out the gradebook or any of those things. She's got her own paperwork to work on." He shrugged nonchalantly, pushing back that feeling growing in his chest when he thought about Sawyer. "He seems eager to learn."

Cynthia snorted. "Can't be any worse than Old Miss Doris— you guys remember her?" Everyone groaned and began telling their best Old Miss Doris substitute story to Kristine, who was new to the school.

Matt finished his lunch and stood. "I've got to run and make copies." Bidding them all goodbye, he made his way across the hall into the workroom.

· · • • • • • • · ·

To: All_Staff_HaysMS

From: Rosa Mendez

Date: August 30

Subject: Morale Building Committee

The Morale Building Committee will meet Friday after school at Gringo's celebrating the end of the first week. Appetizers are half off until six. Email me if you're coming so we can save you a seat.

— — —

Rosa Mendez

Principal's Secretary, Sarah Hays Middle School

· · • • • • • • · ·

Matt spent his eighth period on Friday making copies for the next week for both his and Dorothy's classes, catching up on emails and paperwork. The bell that signaled the end of the day rang right as he stood and erased the day's agenda from his front board and started writing Monday's topic and objectives. He was so busy thinking about what he wanted to write that he missed someone entering his classroom.

"Wow, you're organized."

Turning around, Matt spotted Sawyer standing in the doorway, his beat-up satchel slung over his shoulder, an effortless sort of handsome that Matt could never achieve. "Never hurts to stay one step ahead," he said briskly.

"So I'm learning." Sawyer walked into the room. He picked up an algebra textbook, and grinned as he thumbed through the pages. "Not quite the same as what we're working on."

Matt chuckled. The difference between seventh grade and algebra was vast and deep. "Particularly with your special ed kids. How's that going?" Matt walked toward his desk. One more glance at his computer, checking for any new emails, and then he turned it off with a deep and satisfying sigh.

Sawyer snorted. "It was quite the week. That reminds me." He set his bag on a desk and began pulling out a stack of worksheets. He handed them to Matt with an apologetic look. "I graded everything from yesterday and today. I don't think I've done too much damage with the kids. At least, nothing I can't fix." A wan smile lingered on his face, but the worry was clear in his eyes. "I mean, I don't want to screw things up too bad."

"You'll be okay." Matt grabbed the papers, along with two more thick stacks from his desk, tossing them all into his backpack. "Got any weekend plans?" he asked absently as he turned off the light and walked into the hallway.

"YouTube." Sawyer chuckled. "Gotta learn what I'm teaching next week."

Matt laughed, his face flushing again. *Stop it.* "It's not that bad. You passed seventh grade at some point, I hope."

"I did, but it was a long time ago." Sawyer followed him out into the hallway. "I don't remember learning how to add and subtract integers. I don't even think I could define an integer last week, but here we are."

"Cora's done this for a few years. Let her do the first couple of classes, and you'll pick it up quick," Matt said as they strolled downstairs.

Sawyer agreed. "She's amazing with those kids. All of them, really, but the ones who need the extra help, she's great." Walking down the hall, they saw other teachers all head for the front, shooing stray kids out of the hallway and toward their exits. "How come you're not with the coaches?" Sawyer asked suddenly. "You go down to the gym for the last period of the day, don't you?"

"Friday night football, so no practice on Fridays. The coaches go scout big games for the high school coaches, then they grab a beer afterward. Sometimes I travel with them, but since I've got a lot going on this year, they've given me a bit of a reprieve." The sun was blindingly bright when Sawyer and Matt made it to the front of the school, waving at a few kids who called out their names as they scrambled into their parents' cars.

"Then I guess you're not going to the happy hour," Sawyer said, frowning.

"Me? No, not this time. I've got a paper due by midnight that's not quite complete. But you should go." Matt looked over at Sawyer. Maybe if he wasn't busy, he might indulge in this silly, harmless crush. When was the last time anyone attractive had wandered into this small town and caught his eye? But no, he had responsibilities. "It'll be fun. Order the nachos—you won't be sorry."

Sawyer grinned, his bright blue eyes crinkling as he laughed. "Nachos. Will do." He took a few steps toward the right side of the parking lot. "Hey, Matt. Thanks for all you did for me this week. And last week too. I get that you're super busy and all."

Matt shrugged it off. "Have a good time tonight." He headed toward his truck and, glancing back, saw Sawyer walking toward the bike rack and unlocking a ten-speed bicycle. He chuckled, imagining the man biking down to Gringo's, and for a moment he seriously considered joining them.

But this assignment wouldn't finish itself. Tossing his backpack into the passenger side of his old Ford truck, he started the engine and drove toward his house.

Matt had silenced his phone and left it plugged in its charger while he sat at his desk and worked on his paper, but out of the corner of his eye he noticed the screen light up repeatedly with each new message received. *Must be a hell of a happy hour*, he guessed, coming to a stopping point a little after eight. Once he submitted the paper, Matt closed his laptop and tossed it on his bed, reaching for the phone.

Yeah, there were a lot of messages.

Cora: Miss you, Matt! We had a round in your name. Hope you're studying a lot. Sawyer said you had to finish a paper.

Deanna: Did you know Sawyer used to own a restaurant? He cooks! He's bringing cinnamon rolls on Monday, so drop by my room when you get there.

Daisy: I love Dorothy's sub! Norma said he rides a bike to school each day.

Eva: (sent a picture of several of them, all laughing) Sawyer's hysterical. Wish you were here!

Matt looked at the messages for a long time, not sure what was happening, when it hit him. Oh. *Oh.* Damn.

Sawyer was gay. The cute, new long-term substitute was gay, and in their collective and slightly drunken wisdom, his colleagues wanted him to know. Just in case, you know.

Shit.

September

M att's first kiss with a girl happened at his eighth-grade end-of-the-year dance. He and Tara Houghton slow danced to "I'm With You" by Avril Lavigne and then kissed in a dark hallway. They chatted a few times over the phone that summer, but once school started up in the fall, Matt pushed himself into school and football, working on the ranch on the weekends and deciding he didn't have time for a girlfriend.

Matt's first kiss with a boy happened the weekend after his seventeenth birthday. By then, Matt had come to terms with being gay, but there weren't many openly gay students in his high school. Even if there were, Matt drew little attention to his sexuality. His teachers considered him a good kid—smart, polite, dressed okay, and if the absence of a dating life suggested his sexual orientation, so be it. It didn't hurt that he was a natural athlete, playing all the sports well. His coaches considered Matt a tough son of a bitch, the greatest compliment a semi-closeted gay boy in Texas could accomplish. He could ignore the casual homophobic comments in the locker room and pretend they weren't talking about him.

But one night during his junior year, Matt found himself at a bonfire on Jorge Duarte's family's farm after the district track and field finals. He drank a couple of beers and stole into an empty barn with Derek Marshall, a senior and one of the few "out and proud" boys at his high school. They jerked each other off and then sat in the hay, holding hands and talking shit about people they knew and life in Estella. The next day, Matt called and told Derek he didn't want any kind of relationship, and they were both cool about it. Life changed little after that; Matt had a few close friends who knew about him, and for senior prom, he went with a group of friends and had a great time.

Being gay would never define him. His grandparents never asked, and if they suspected, they kept it to themselves.

Matt met Justin, his first serious boyfriend, when he was nineteen and a freshman at the University of Texas. A friend of a friend, they dated on and off for a year until Matt's grandmother got sick, and he took a semester off to help at home. Since then, he'd dated a couple of guys here and there along the way, but nothing important, and no one serious since he started working full time as a teacher. Despite some initial misgivings when he'd first gotten the job, Matt had never felt like an outcast or outsider because of his sexuality at Hays and guessed that most people on campus knew about his sexual orientation, and just didn't care about it. Aside from the occasional chatter about setting him up with their gay cousins, the lack of conversation about it was unusual, but he wasn't a flamboyant queen. No one discussed it, and Matt was fine with that. One day he'd have time for a relationship, but not now.

Absolutely not now.

•••••••••

Spending the last period of the day working with the athletes always boosted Matt's mood. Something about the physical activity and camaraderie with the coaches, mixed with the September sunshine, helped reduce any frustration Matt had picked up from spending the day teaching. One afternoon in mid-September he walked into the locker room and heard all the kids changing into their practice gear, laughing and joking with each other. It reminded him of his own football days when he was a kid, some of the best times in his life. Turning the corner, he spotted Paul and Clint in the coaches' office huddled over the large white board and walked over to join them.

"Making changes already?" he asked, curious as they glared at the board, covered in football plays, Xs, and arrows. "I thought things were good. Eighth grade won their first two scrimmages, right?"

Paul shook his head, and Matt could see how upset he was. "We lost Jason Trevino. The family is moving to California."

Matt stared back and forth, unconvinced. Jason was in his third period math class, smart as a whip, and a hell of a quarterback. "Are you sure?"

Clint nodded. "He came by a few minutes ago to drop off his gear and say goodbye. Parents are withdrawing him right now."

"Fuck." Matt felt gutted and understood their long faces. "He's a great kid. Gonna miss him. I had him in class today—he said nothing about this."

"Gonna miss his right arm." Paul snorted. "I think he didn't tell us this was all going on because it upset him too." He looked over at the whiteboard again, shaking his head. "We just don't have anybody else even close to being ready to quarterback the team like that kid."

Right at that moment, the boys rushed out of the locker room doors and out to the football field. "I'll go with them to the field." Clint reached for his old fishing hat and sunglasses. Matt didn't miss the look that passed between the two coaches. "Catch you guys in a bit."

After Clint left, Matt turned back to Paul. "What was that all about?" he asked, worried.

"Well, you know," Paul began. "We were talking. You know, we appreciate how much you've got on your plate right now, having to babysit the new teacher and your own classes you're taking. Maybe it's time to step back and not worry about helping us out during eighth period this year."

Matt's eyes widened as Paul talked. "No way. I'm fine. Thanks for thinking of me, but really. I need this time with you guys. I look forward to it each and every day."

Paul didn't seem convinced. "You're sure?"

Matt punched his shoulder twice. "C'mon, let's go. We gotta find a new quarterback."

It was after six, the sun hanging low in the sky, when Matt left the locker room and headed toward his truck. He spotted Sawyer walking his bike past the school toward the crosswalk.

Once he'd learned Sawyer was also gay, Matt had pulled back on their burgeoning friendship. A harmless crush was one thing, but lusting after the only other gay man at his place of employment was asking for trouble. But ignoring the man was an asshole move as well, Matt knew that, so he walked toward Sawyer, giving a slight wave. "You're here late. Is everything okay?"

Sawyer nodded. "Getting ready for tomorrow. I guess the key to avoiding long lines at the copy machine is staying late."

"Or getting here early," Matt added. "Let me know if you need any help."

"You already do too much."

"It's my job to help you." Guilt surged through Matt, and he didn't like how he'd been coming across. "I'm sorry if I made you feel like it was burdensome." How much complaining had he been doing if this was coming from both the coaches and Sawyer? "So, how are the classes going?"

Sawyer shrugged. "I'll be honest, I wasn't thrilled with the test grades on two step equations this afternoon. Cora and I had a long talk after school. I think we need to go over them again tomorrow, maybe let them take that section of the test again before we start inequalities."

"Maybe you could split the class into two groups. Take the kids did that did alright, and give them an independent activity to work on while you help the kids who didn't get it." Matt stopped and grinned. "Or better still, let the kids who got it pair up with the ones who didn't."

Sawyer nodded, understanding spreading on his face. "They listen to each other better sometimes. And it'll be an immense help in those classes I teach by myself."

"It's worth a shot."

"Thanks, man. I'm going to call Cora and see what she thinks." He smiled at Matt. "You have a good night, okay?"

"You too."

Sawyer turned to leave.

"Hey," Matt called out, stepping closer. "Look, I get here pretty early most mornings. I know you're picking up the math on your own, but if you ever want my help—you know, figuring out how to approach the lesson—I can give you any tips I know on how to explain it more clearly, or little tricks of the trade."

Sawyer took a breath. "You sure? I don't want to be any more of a bother."

Matt shook his head. "Stop by my room when you get here. I'll look over what you're doing tomorrow and see what we can come up with."

Sawyer's smile was quick and bright. "You bet. I'll see you then. And..." He looked down at his feet, almost shy. "Thanks."

· · • • • • • • · ·

Sawyer shook his head and walked away from the whiteboard, handing his dry erase marker back to Matt. "This is awful. I don't want to teach it. I'm calling Curtis and quitting right now, I mean it."

Matt sighed, ignoring Sawyer's overreacting as he erased his first example off the board. Teaching inequalities was grueling in the best of circumstances, something he'd never enjoyed. Explaining how to model inequalities on a number line when you yourself weren't comfortable with the concept was a nightmare. "It's not a barrel of laughs, yeah. But it's an expectation of the seventh-grade curriculum. Equations and inequalities." He gave Sawyer a knowing look. "You can teach them. You can do it," Matt told him. "And soon, I hope, because the bell is going to ring in fifteen minutes."

Sawyer glanced up at him, disbelief in his eyes. "I mean, equations, that makes sense. X equals three. It all balances out, all the numbers on one side, the letter on the other. I can explain that. I can show that on a number line. But inequalities?" He shook his head again. "I'm on their side. I've never had to use this as an adult. It's useless."

Matt frowned. He taught thirteen-year-olds; he could teach this twenty-something. "Okay, watch. You cook, right?"

Sawyer's lips quirked. "I've occasionally fried up some bacon."

Matt stared. "Right," he began. "Okay, so let's say you're making bacon for breakfast, and each of us will eat at least four pieces." Matt set up a problem on the whiteboard and began solving, watching to see if Sawyer was following along. He held out the dry erase marker. "Solve it."

Sawyer grinned at him. "I'm still figuring out how I'm making breakfast for you." He snickered, folding his arms.

"Stop." Matt hung his head back, but he couldn't help grinning at that comment. "How do you answer this?" Matt ignored how the man's fingers glided over his as he took the marker. Sawyer erased the top line from the equals sign and replaced it with a greater-than sign. "Now the number line."

Sawyer drew a crude number line on the board, hash marks for numbers one through ten. "What numbers satisfy this rule?" Matt pointed at the board. "Draw it."

Sawyer looked at the board carefully. "You put a closed circle under the eight—"

"Why?" Matt asked.

Sawyer pointed at the line under the greater-than sign. "Because it could be equal to eight."

"Yes." Matt picked up another marker and drew a closed circle under the eight. "Next? What other numbers make this inequality true?"

"Nine and ten," Sawyer answered.

Matt drew an arrow in that direction, then looked at Sawyer. "That wasn't so hard."

Sawyer shook his head again. "It's easy when you're standing up there and pointing out the obvious."

"And it shall be easy for them when you do the same."

Sawyer scrubbed his face with one hand. "For the record, I didn't have to do this as a kid, and I turned out okay."

"For fuck's sake, Sawyer," Matt murmured as he erased the board. "Don't tell them that."

··········

The eighth-grade football team's first district game of the year was at home. Since Clint coached the seventh-grade team who played away, Matt worked with Paul on the sidelines. It was a hot Texas September afternoon, so besides helping take care of the defense, Matt made certain the kids stayed hydrated when they ran off the field.

It was a good crowd too, the bleachers filled with parents and a sizable student section who came out to cheer on their team. They'd been trying out a new quarterback, but the team was still down by ten at halftime. Matt sat down, checking his phone and texting Clint to see how the seventh graders were faring.

"Coach?" Matt glanced up and saw Melissa, one of his students from first period standing in front of him, holding two soft drinks and two bags of chips. "Mr. Evans said to give these to the coaches." Melissa glanced over at Coach Paul before smiling at him and running back to the tent.

Student Council always sold concessions at athletic events, and he spotted Laverne, the Student Council sponsor, underneath a white canopy tent by the bleachers, watching over the students as they made their sales. Then he noticed another familiar face. A familiar person, at least—Sawyer helping one girl roll an ice chest over to their tent. Matt waved over, grinning when Sawyer waved back.

Paul nudged him, as if reading his mind. "Your boy can't say no to any of those ladies, can he? They got him working hard as a mule over there."

Matt laughed, nudging aside that strange disquiet Paul's words awakened, the notion of Sawyer and the female teachers, and Sawyer being characterized as "his boy." "He seems to be popular with the staff."

Paul nodded. "With the kids too. My Brandy's in his class and told us he's doing a good job. Tries hard, doesn't yell to make his voice heard. Kids respect that," he added. "I mean, I was hoping she'd be older before crushing on some long-haired guy with tattoos all over his arms, but kids these days. Anyway, I expect you'll be glad when their actual teacher gets back. Six more weeks?"

Six weeks until he's gone. Like a punch to his gut, knowing Sawyer was leaving in a matter of weeks. "I guess so, yeah," Matt answered, glancing once more at the concession tent before looking up to watch the team settling back into place as the scoreboard buzzed. Time for the second half.

···•••••···

"I'm sorry to hear about the game."

Matt glanced into his refrigerator, scanning the shelves for something quick to eat. "I know, Grandma, but we'll win next time. The kids look good this year. They just need some time to mesh together."

"Maybe we can come see one of your games. You know how your grandpa likes football."

He pulled out some sliced ham and began making himself a sandwich. "Yeah, I bet Grandpa would drive you into town to watch a game. Well, as soon as the weather gets nicer. It's still so hot out." Matt heard the ping that signaled an incoming text. "I'll talk to you tomorrow. Love you too." After ending the call, he looked down at the incoming call's number.

The Portland area code made him grin.

Sawyer: *Can we meet in the morning? I want to go over some ideas for test review I came up with.*

Matt: *Sounds good, see you then. Thanks for the sodas and chips.*

Sawyer: *No worries. Sorry about the loss today. Better luck next week.*

········

Matt read Sawyer's last response, then set his phone down. Six weeks until Sawyer left, then Matt could get his life back to normal.

········

A month into school, Matt felt like he'd found an efficient routine. Gym, coffee, school, then coaching. After making it home, he worked on grad class assignments, grading, answering emails and texts before calling his grandmother and then going to bed. It kept his day full and active, but Matt liked that productive feeling. Occasionally he skipped the gym in order to get to school even earlier to get his shit done before meeting Sawyer for their own math lessons.

Those days were his favorite.

The biggest surprise of the year so far, in fact, had been Lopez's math class. Matt had expected to spend many extra hours each week working on the lesson plans and answer keys for that class, but after that first month at work, Sawyer had stepped up and taken on as much responsibility as he could within the purview of being a substitute. Sawyer graded all the assignments, taking a considerable chunk of work Matt had expected to do. Sawyer also started asking the other math teachers for help when he wasn't certain how to approach a lesson.

In fact, Matt hadn't seen Sawyer much at all this week, other than standing at the doorway between periods as they greeted their students entering the classroom.

"He spends his weekends working out all the problems and making his own keys, to reinforce his learning," Cora mentioned as she dropped off grades for him to enter. Sawyer's work ethic impressed the hell out of Matt.

But the closer Matt and Sawyer got as friends, the more awkward he felt. Sawyer sometimes wore this blue chambray shirt the exact same color as his eyes, and he looked real good in it.

Real good.

Occasionally Matt heard Sawyer's cheerful laughter booming down the hallway. He admired the natural way Sawyer connected with the students between classes.

But worst of all was Jeans Day.

On Fridays, the teachers could wear jeans with their Hays Hawks school shirts. Last week, Matt found himself distracted during the monthly department meeting before school, watching Sawyer walk into Deanna's room with homemade pastries, wearing a pair of washed-out blue jeans that fit him snug around the hips.

It was fucking distracting.

A old college friend had once told him it was rude to jerk off to your friends, and yet Sawyer's face and body snuck into Matt's fantasies when he touched himself in the shower.

· · · • • · • · · ·

One morning in late September, Matt arrived at the gym a few minutes later than usual and realized someone had beaten him to the rowing machine. Tall, from the looks of it, with a ponytail tucked into a top bun. Matt could only see the man from behind, and he knew it wasn't Sawyer, but he couldn't stop gawking, listening as the other man exhaled loud with each stroke.

Thinking. Wondering. Imagining Sawyer making those grunting sounds.

Fuck.

· · · • • · • · · ·

Matt saw the text notification and paused the show he was watching, reaching for his phone.

Sawyer: *Sorry to text so late but I got some news for you. I forgot to tell you, I missed you all day. I mean I missed seeing you. Anyway, I got a new kid in my 6th period.*

Matt: Really? How many is that now?

Sawyer: 24 I think, but that's not the news. This kid stayed after school to work on putting his spiral notebook together and I asked about how he was doing, new school and all. He said he was okay but his brother was sad because he used to be the quarterback at his old school and had to leave his team.

Matt: 8th grade?

Sawyer: Yeah. Said his bro hasn't said anything to coaches because he's still mad about moving. Name's DeShaun Edwards. He's in Sylvia's class. Talk to him. Might be the answer to your prayers.

Matt: I'll go find him tomorrow. Thanks!

Sawyer: Anytime. Go Hawks lol

Matt set his phone down and turned the TV off, no longer interested in finishing his show. He brushed his teeth and went to bed. Resting his head on his pillow, he stared at the ceiling for a long moment. Sawyer really was a good guy.

Matt wondered what kind of guy appealed to him. He wondered what Sawyer's last boyfriend looked like, and why they'd split up.

He wondered what Sawyer looked like without those blue jeans on.

October

· · · · · · · · · ·

I n the blink of an eye, the first quarter was over. Panicking students were suddenly turning in piles of missing assignments, and Matt had to enter all the grades for both his and Sawyer's classes. The teachers had until Monday to enter their grades, but his grandmother had asked him to come to the ranch over the weekend and help with the winter hay delivery, and he didn't want the grades looming over his head all weekend. But during eighth period, Matt realized he was missing grades from two of Sawyer's classes, so he walked down the hall to ask about them.

A paper sign taped to C106 said the class was in the cafeteria. Curious. Matt jogged downstairs to see what was going on. Turning the corner off the stairwell, he spotted several students taping brown-and-gold streamers to the cafeteria's glass walls, while other students helped custodians push the long tables and chairs to the side of the room to set up a dance floor.

Of course, Sawyer had offered to help. As he neared the cafeteria, Matt noticed him on the far-right side of the large room, assisting a couple of students make concession price list signs on poster boards.

"Hey," Matt said. "I found you."

"You found me," Sawyer repeated with a smirk, finishing his poster and holding it up to the others for inspection. Sawyer rarely wore his hair down, but today he had a few strands pulled back on top into a small ponytail, the rest of it flowing free and brushing his shoulders. Looking up at Matt, Sawyer continued, "Be careful. If you stand around too long or ask what's going on, you're going to get enlisted into helping decorate for the dance."

"Is that what happened here?" Matt stepped back as another group of kids walked by, carrying cases of soft drinks and boxes of chips and candy, setting them all up behind two long tables. "You cannot say no to anyone, can you?"

"Apparently not," Sawyer agreed. "In my defense, the eighth period class is ahead of the other classes because they're exceptional." Sawyer reached out and high-fived one of the boys. "We didn't want to get any further ahead, so here we are, as a reward. Also, I don't remember dances being this cool when I was a kid, and I was curious. It looks like it's going to be a fun time."

"Mr. Ruiz," Angela York called out to him as she approached. She'd been their PTA president for the past four years. But her youngest was an eighth grader this year and leaving for high school, and Angela was finishing her reign with a bang. "Would you mind helping us with the tables?" she asked. "Hard as these kids are trying, we're running out of time and could use your free labor and leg muscles." She smiled at Sawyer. "You too, Mr. Evans."

"Absolutely." Glancing down at his phone, Matt saw they still had a few minutes left before the end of the day. Matt rolled up his sleeves, and soon he and Sawyer were moving tables over to the side. After that, he helped the kids finish setting up the concession area, arranging the candies and taping signs up to the cafeteria walls and on the front of the tables. "See, if you put the ice chests with the drinks over here," Matt said, pointing at the far-left side of their table, "you won't have that condensation dripping all over the money and the rest of the food."

The girls looked impressed. "That's smart."

"Not my first rodeo." Matt laughed. He looked up as the final bell rang, signaling the end of the school day. Soon the cafeteria swarmed with kids running for their backpacks and binders. They poured out into the hallways and joined their friends as they rambled down the hall toward their lockers. "Are you staying for the dance?" Matt asked. He turned to see if Sawyer followed him.

"Yeah." Sawyer nodded and waved at Mrs. York, to let her know he'd be right back. "I told Dan I'd take pictures for the yearbook for him. His daughter's scout troop is camping overnight somewhere this weekend, and he couldn't make it tonight. But I need to get my bag and turn off my computer." Sawyer looked over at Matt as they made their way down the crowded hall and up the stairs, students excited at the prospect of the impending school dance. "Are you staying?"

"Can't. Heading to the ranch this weekend." They reached their hallway, and Matt opened his door. He turned and leaned against the doorway. "They're having hay delivered for the cows. I guess they need to eat this winter." Matt rolled his eyes. "Apparently they also need my free labor."

"And your leg muscles." Sawyer grinned. "Well, you and the cows have a pleasant weekend. You've earned it. I'll see you on Monday."

"You too, Sawyer."

Sawyer walked down toward his classroom, turning back and looking one last time at Matt before he unlocked his classroom door and stepped inside.

Matt was halfway to the ranch when he remembered why he'd gone looking for Sawyer in the first place—the missing grades. Oh *well*, he decided. They'd just have to get together Monday morning.

········

"As we all know, this weekend is the annual Fall Food Fest," Deanna announced as she closed out the end of the month department meeting. "Historically, this has been the most successful fundraiser for the Hays Middle School Math Club, and I expect this year to be no exception." She held up a sign-up sheet. "We've got a cold front blowing in tomorrow, so— Please stop laughing, Mr. Evans, I can see you mocking me, but highs in the low fifties is brisk and chilly, and I am choosing to ignore you. Alex is changing his donation of soft drinks to include hot cocoa makings. Great idea, Alex. Sylvia is bringing her pumpkin bars and lemon bars, and I've got my mom's famous brownie recipe—"

"The one with the cookie dough mixed in?" Sylvia asked, tapping her pencil on her desk.

"That very recipe." Deanna smiled proudly "Even though she's gone, Dorothy has sent money to buy napkins, plates, and cups. Sawyer has kindly offered to make us gourmet cupcakes." All the teachers glanced around at each other, excited at this prospect. Then Deanna glanced over at Matt. "We know you're pretty busy this year, Matt, so you're off the hook if you don't have time to help."

Fuck. He felt that brief stab of guilt right between the eyes. "I'll come up with something." Matt reached for the sign-up sheet. "And I will be there for sure tomorrow to help sell, as long as you need me."

"You could help me with the cupcakes." Sawyer glanced over at him. "I could make even more if I've got help with frosting and decorating them while I'm baking." Sawyer looked over at Matt, a wry smile on his face. "If you have time tonight."

Matt considered it. He'd planned on going out to one of the high school football games with Paul, but shame and guilt won out. Guilt and something else. "I've got time."

Deanna's face broke out into a broad smile. "Fabulous. I'm not gonna lie, I think Sawyer's cupcakes are going to steal the show tomorrow. I've had several staff members ask me about them already." She added Matt's name to the sign-up sheet and set it on her desk. "The festival starts at eleven AM sharp, so have your food here before then or bring them to my house this evening. Please remind the Math Club kids in your classes what time they need to be here tomorrow with their baked goods, or if they're helping us sell. We're setting up tables in the faculty parking lot." The first bell of the day began to chime, signaling the end of the meeting and the start of first period. "Have a great day, everyone."

During third period, Matt felt his phone vibrate.

Sawyer: *I didn't mean to put you on the spot this morning. If you can't make it, I won't say anything to anyone. You can still take credit for helping.*

Matt was tempted. But no, he needed to help. Also, he wanted to see where Sawyer lived.

Matt: *No, I can come. I need to help. Send me your address. What time?*
Sawyer: *Shady Creek RV park, #26, any time after 5.*

· · · ● · ● · ● · · ·

The Shady Creek RV park sat on the edge of town, up Highway 183, leading toward Austin. Matt arrived at half past five, pulling into the park and slowing at the first intersection, re-reading the directions Sawyer had sent him. Enter the park, make a right, another right, and a left at the playground, parking next to a large blue pickup truck parked behind a shiny silver Airstream. The familiar ten-speed leaned against the front of the trailer, close to a small barbecue grill, patio table, and a couple of flower pots. Two crudely carved pumpkins decorated the ground around the steps up to the RV's front door.

Interesting. Matt stepped out of his truck, carrying a six pack of Shiner Bock, and heard someone calling his name. Turning his head, Matt saw Sawyer waving at him from an adjacent trailer, wearing jeans and a Hays Hawks hoodie. Sawyer finished speaking to an older woman standing on her porch and hugged her goodbye before making his way toward Matt. "You found me."

"I found you," Matt said, glancing around and handing Sawyer the beer. Several of the RVs had been parked for years, from the looks of it, with more space between them than Matt had expected. The RV next to Sawyer had a picnic table in front, a Texas flag, and a satellite dish mounted to the roof. "You know, I've lived in this town almost all my life, and I've never been here, to this trailer park. It's bigger than I thought." Glancing at Sawyer's shiny silver Airstream, he nodded in appreciation, noticing the hook-ups on the back to the RV park's water and electricity system.

"It's a nice little place," Sawyer replied. "It's quiet, and there's a creek that runs behind the park. Sometimes I see kids fishing out there." He stepped up and into the trailer, holding the door open for Matt and closing it after Matt stepped inside. It made Matt smile, seeing an entire house packed into a long silver tube, but here it was. "Please, let me give you the grand tour." He pointed to the right of the front door. "Living area." Matt saw a small sofa and table, television mounted on a cabinet, shelves close to the top covered in cookbooks and plants. A small Yorkie stretched out lazily on the sofa, sitting up and yawning when she noticed they had a guest. "This is Biscuit," he said, stroking her back as she approached them. "She's harmless, mostly."

"She's cute." Matt reached out and petted her silky ears. "I saw her in one of your videos." He'd spent the better part of an afternoon a couple of weeks prior watching Sawyer's videos on YouTube. It'd been...enlightening. On camera, Sawyer was utterly charming, with his infectious smile and enthusiasm when he talked about food and traveling. Matt could see how he'd make a popular substitute teacher. "I liked the one where you made chile con carne, in New Mexico."

Sawyer closed his eyes. "With the really spicy—"

"Yeah." Matt laughed. "That red chile sauce looked great."

"Hot as fuck. They don't joke about the heat over there. I think my video on the Hatch chiles was better. Did a big ole chile relleno if I remember right."

Matt had watched that one as well but didn't mention seeing it. He'd focused on Sawyer's enormous hands, so delicate when chopping up the cheese and battering the peppers, quick and sure. Matt had been mesmerized, but Sawyer was his friend, that's all. "I'll have to check it out later."

He glanced down the other side of the RV as Sawyer grinned and continued the tour. "Bedroom and bathroom," he said, stepping to the left and pointing to the other end of the trailer. Matt could see a door that led to the bathroom, and a small writing desk across from a queen-sized bed, neatly made and covered in pillows. "And then my kitchen." Sawyer held his hands out in front of his stove, pride in his voice.

"This is amazing." Matt looked down at what he could only describe as a gourmet mini kitchen. One side had a three-burner gas stove next to a small sink and counter, a magnetic knife rack against the wall above a magnetic spice rack. The other side had a large butcher block counter and stools. Shelves above a miniature fridge held nested mixing bowls and measuring cups. "You know, I saw some pictures of this on your blog, but in person, it's even more impressive." Peering closer, Matt saw cabinets filled with high-quality ingredients, exposed shelves holding cast-iron cookware, and several baking pans. "Did you have to custom order all of this?"

"Parts of it. Most of these have gas ovens anyway, but I upgraded mine."

"It's unique." From end to end, Matt guessed the trailer was about thirty feet, with no wasted space, and yet it didn't feel crowded. Matt wouldn't even guess how much this must've cost, along with that big truck outside. There was a story behind this. "I appreciate you letting me help you tonight. It just slipped my mind."

"I think you've helped me enough this year to earn me doing this for the both of us." Sawyer smiled at him, warmth in his eyes. "But I'll admit that having company tonight while I work on this is much appreciated."

Sawyer grabbed a beer for each of them, handing one to Matt, and then pulled out a tablet and scrolled through until he found what he was looking for, setting it up against the counter where he could read a recipe. "When I talked to Deanna, I tossed around the idea of fall flavors, since it's October and all. A little change of pace from plain old vanilla and chocolate, you know? This is what I was thinking." Sawyer leaned against the counter, talking with his hands as he described the cupcakes. "First, caramel apple with a vanilla cake and an apple compote center, with caramel buttercream frosting and maybe a caramel drizzle. We can also do Black Forest cupcakes. They're my favorite," Sawyer admitted. "Dark, rich chocolate cake with a black cherry compote filling, with cream cheese buttercream and chocolate shavings and cherry on top." With a mischievous smirk, he added, "We can do those two, but I also happened to have all the ingredients for a pumpkin cheesecake cupcake. It'd be a moist pumpkin cake with cheesecake filling, and pumpkin-pie-spiced buttercream and graham cracker sprinkles on top." Matt's eyes widened, and Sawyer stopped. "What's wrong?" he asked. "No good?"

"Dude." Matt stared at him, incredulous. "Those sound amazing. Are you sure you want to go through all that trouble? This is a middle school bake sale, for fuck's sake."

But Sawyer smiled back at him, this brilliant light in his blue eyes as he spoke. "Matt, this is what I love to do. Honestly, I've been waiting for an excuse to make these."

Matt still wasn't convinced. "You're sure?" he asked one more time.

Sawyer opened a few cabinets and started bringing down ingredients. When he stretched, his hoodie rode up, and Matt spotted the edges of a lower back tattoo. He'd seen more of it on one of Sawyer's videos, one where Sawyer had been running on the side of some mountain in Colorado.

The day Matt had discovered he had a thing for back tattoos.

"Trust me, this is going to be fun." Sawyer looked over at Matt, lingering a moment too long for Matt's comfort. "We're going to cheat a little with the fillings, but they'll still be delicious. Have a seat." Sawyer pointed him to the butcher-block table across from the stove. After he sat down, Sawyer started handing him cans of pumpkin, apple, and cherry fillings, along with a can opener. "Get those open, and then I'm going to set you up to make all the buttercream." Again, Matt's face must've shown shock, because Sawyer walked up close to him, resting a hand on Matt's cheek, patting it softly. "You'll be great."

His skin burned where Sawyer touched him—not because the act itself was sexual; quite the opposite. It was a soft, friendly gesture, but it'd been a long time since anyone had stepped close to Matt like that, right in his space, controlling the situation. For someone as in control of his life as Matt was, this touch set every nerve on fire.

He could think about that later. Now it was cupcake time.

Matt opened the cans as directed, then watched as Sawyer plugged in his large stand mixer and pulled out canisters of flour and sugar and other ingredients, along with two of the beer bottles, opening them and offering one to Matt. "You said you lived here your entire life. What was that like?" Sawyer took a sip, then reached up onto the shelves and pulled down several large stainless-steel mixing bowls.

"Well, almost my entire life. I spent four years in Austin at the university," Matt said, opening the cans. He set them aside, waiting for more instructions, watching as Sawyer opened a cabinet and handed Matt several boxes of powdered sugar and vanilla extract. "All this?"

Sawyer added a small container of milk and several sticks of butter to his pile of things on the table. "Well, for now. We'll see how it goes." He smiled brightly at Matt. "Start opening these. You'll need the mixer as soon as I'm done over here. So, keep going with your story. You came back here when you graduated. What was that about?" Sawyer measured out his dry ingredients and then wet ingredients, breaking eggs into the bowl and mixing everything together into something that resembled vanilla batter.

Matt had been watching Sawyer throw this all together, but that question pulled him back to reality. He took a deep breath, thinking back to that day, the one that had changed his life forever. "Right before I turned twenty, they diagnosed my grandmother with cancer."

"Oh, shit." Sawyer stopped the mixer to look at him. "I'm so sorry."

"Yeah." Matt nodded. "It was bad. We thought we might lose her for a while. Anyway, Sabrina was still in high school, and they needed help with the ranch and getting her to appointments and just..." Matt shrugged. "I took a semester off, and when I got back, I changed my major."

"From what to what?"

"Aerospace engineering to education."

Sawyer had been separating cupcake liners and inserting them into the pan, but now he looked up. "Wait, what? Why did you do that?"

Matt reached for the second cupcake pan and helped, inserting more liners. "I needed something where I could get a job right away—"

Sawyer's eyes narrowed, turning to face Matt. "And engineering wouldn't do that?"

"You see many jobs for aerospace engineers in Estella?"

"Matt." Sawyer put one hand on his hip. "You're literally right down the road from Houston."

"And," Matt continued, speaking slowly, "I needed to be close to them. Down-the-street kind of close." It was hard to explain now how it felt, nineteen years old and worried about losing the woman who'd raised him, who'd given up everything to take care of them. "It was the right decision."

Sawyer whistled low. "You gave up a lot, Matt."

"Yeah." Matt nodded. "But it's what family does."

"Some families, I guess." Sawyer reached up and turned on a small speaker, indie rock playing quiet in the background as they worked. Pulling out a small scoop, he quickly filled the two cupcake pans with vanilla batter and put them in the oven, setting his timer. "Your turn to use the mixer while I clean up over here and get started on batter number two." Sawyer moved the tablet over to where Matt could read the buttercream recipe: add butter, add sugar, add a little milk. "I made caramel earlier so it'd be cool for you to use it," he added, setting a small bowl in front of Matt.

"That's it?" Matt looked up from the tablet. "Just mix this up?"

"Crazy, right?" Sawyer helped Matt get started on creaming the butter and adding the sugar a little at a time.

Matt smirked, as it all seemed to come together at the end, light and fluffy. "I did it," he said proudly, sliding a finger along the edge of the bowl, tasting it. Sawyer watched him lick the tip of his finger and chuckled. "What? It's good!"

"I hope it is. I mean, I'm not surprised you can follow a recipe. It's that engineering background." Sawyer handed Matt a piping bag and a spoon. "So why aerospace? Did you want to be an astronaut or something?"

Matt bit his lip in contemplation before he answered. "No, not really. I mean, that would be cool, but that wasn't what interested me. I liked robotics when I was a kid, and growing up, I remember seeing those Mars rovers and I wanted to be a part of that." Building machines that would live and work on another planet.

"And now you're in grad school, right? Do you ever think about going back and trying to get into robotics now? Change it over to a program that'll get you back into that field?"

"It's too late. The people who get into those programs have master's degrees in aerospace engineering and years of experience by my age. They work at Boston Dynamics or Bluefin. JPL. Places like that." Looking over at Sawyer, Matt shrugged. "But I took what life gave me and made an alternative plan, and now I've got a goal I think is worth working toward."

"They said you want to be the superintendent."

"I do. I think it is a reasonable goal, and one that'd let me leap into a bigger district, a bigger city one day when I'm done here." He hesitated, then added, "Maybe move to Austin and help shape education policy at the state level." That idea had started poking at him since his graduate classes had begun. He hadn't mentioned it to anyone else. "I think I'd be good at that."

"Wow." Sawyer seemed surprised. "But...what about teaching?"

"What about it?"

"I thought you liked it. You've got the knack," Sawyer said.

Matt shrugged. "It was never in my plan, not forever."

Sawyer looked like he wanted to ask more, but didn't. Instead, he reached for a big spoon and helped Matt scoop the frosting into a piping bag, then picked the mixer back up and set it up at his counter. He began working on chocolate batter. "What was it like, growing up on the ranch? Sounds like a great place to be a kid, outside with the animals and that beautiful land."

"We weren't on the ranch all the time." Sawyer had navigated them into personal territory, and Matt trod carefully. "My grandparents raised my sister Sabrina and me, I guess that's not a secret. When we were little, my mom lived with us too." Sawyer's eyebrows went up. But he didn't speak, waiting for Matt to continue. "One time she took off to get a job in

California." He shrugged. "She never came back for any longer than a couple of days to visit."

"Not even when your grandma got sick?" Matt shook his head. "Fuck," Sawyer murmured. "That sucks, man."

"I can't say it surprised any of us. Truth is," Matt began, then paused, not sure how to explain what it felt like—or rather, why he didn't think about it anymore. "I don't remember the day she left, because she left us a lot, coming and going whenever she got a new job or met a new guy. But I remember the day when I realized she wouldn't ever be coming back." Matt watched Sawyer scoop apple pie filling into another piping bag. "Anyway, we had a house in town when Sabrina and I were kids. My grandpa would go to the ranch a couple of times a week, and then we'd all go on the weekends and stay there. There was an old house there, the one my grandma grew up in. Then after Sabrina graduated, they built a nicer house on the land, and that's where they live now."

"What a great legacy." Sawyer leaned back and smiled, as if the idea made him happy. "You don't want to take over the ranch? Go live on the land when your grandpa retires?"

"Oh no," Matt answered. "That's my sister. Sabrina loves the land, and she has this calling. She's the one who's going to take over."

A timer went off, and Sawyer pulled the first batch of cupcakes out of the oven, arranging them on a pan and setting them in the mini-fridge to cool. He lined the pans with new cupcake liners and began scooping his chocolate batter into them. Soon those were in the oven. Matt got up and washed his bowls, gathered his ingredients together and, with Sawyer's help, started on his chocolate buttercream.

Once the first batch of vanilla cupcakes cooled, Sawyer piped some of the apple pie filling into the cupcakes. After giving Matt a quick tutorial on how to frost the cupcakes, they began a little assembly line. "So," Sawyer began, resuming their earlier conversation, "you said you had a plan, a timeline. What is it?" He looked up, eyes widening. "Tell me you don't have a spreadsheet. You're not *that* person. Are you? Are you that person?"

Matt pretended he hadn't heard that (because he did have a spreadsheet, thank you very much) but smiled anyway as he started piping vanilla frosting on his cupcakes, pleased with how professional they looked. "Maybe. The quick version is I want to finish my Master's in Educational Leadership, then work my way up in administration, first at a school for four years and then at the district level for another four to five years. I should make superintendent somewhere by forty."

"That's...specific." Sawyer's face was hard to read. He took the mixer back and began the batter for the last batch of cupcakes.

"Yeah." Matt looked over at Sawyer. "I'm right on schedule too." Something about his plans bothered Sawyer, but Matt didn't understand how, or why he felt so defensive about it. "Okay, enough about me. What are you doing here in this little podunk Texas town?" he asked, turning the tables on Sawyer.

"Um." Sawyer hesitated, measuring flour and sugar. "Well, you know about the restaurant. It wasn't working anymore, so we sold—for an excellent price, mind you. I took the money and bought this." His hand waved around his trailer. "Then I picked up the truck and started traveling. I wanted to get out of Oregon and see the rest of the west."

"What wasn't working?"

A moment passed before Sawyer answered. "My partner and me. I guess us working together wasn't what he thought it was going to be. Running the restaurant was a lot of pressure, and he didn't... Well, I couldn't do it alone, so we sold."

"And then you just left?" Matt looked incredulous. "That's crazy. I can't imagine what it's like to pick up and leave whenever you're done with a place." Sawyer looked up when Matt said this. "I didn't mean that in any sort of way. It's just...it looks like fun, traveling and cooking and camping out." But Matt couldn't do that. It wasn't in him to leave his family.

At least, not right now.

Matt glanced over at the stove again. "How do you film yourself?"

Sawyer opened a low cabinet and pulled out camera equipment, stands and cords all bundled up together. "This camera records me from above. Then there's this one here." Sawyer held up an expensive-looking camera. "This gets perched on a tripod and records me from the side. And that clips over here, so I have extra lighting, a microphone, and *voila.*"

"It's quite the set-up. I'm impressed," Matt said.

Sawyer flushed an adorable pink. "Thank you."

Soon the chocolate cupcakes finished baking, and Sawyer put the pumpkin ones into the oven. Matt helped shift the vanilla cupcakes onto the table, making room for the chocolate ones cooling in the fridge. They'd figured out a rhythm to get this done, the two of them moving around the small kitchen with an unexpected familiarity, and Matt surprised himself with how much of the baking process he picked up. "You talk to your family? What do they think about all this?" he asked as they began filling and frosting the chocolate cupcakes.

"They're busy people." There was an uncharacteristic tightness in Sawyer's voice, so Matt didn't press the topic.

Finally, the pumpkin cupcakes were cooling, and together they worked on the final decorations. "You mean, caramel is just sugar and water? That's it?" Matt watched Sawyer spooning little wisps of the sticky strands over the vanilla cupcakes as he added cherries and graham cracker bits to the chocolate and pumpkin cupcakes. "It's like magic."

"Almost." Sawyer looked satisfied as he looked over Matt's work. "You're doing a superb job."

It was almost ten when they finished packing the cupcakes into boxes. "I can't believe we made these. They're too pretty to eat." Matt stared at the large cardboard boxes, several dozen packed and ready to go. "I don't care what you said, I know you spent your own money on this."

Sawyer shrugged. "Deanna gave me a little seed money for ingredients. Besides, it's all for a good cause, right?"

"On behalf of the Hays Middle School Math Club, thank you."

Sawyer handed Matt a piece of leftover chocolate cupcake.

He took a bite, groaning in pleasure. "I can't believe we made these."

"We did." Sawyer grinned and ate broken bits of cake. "You were a great baking assistant, Matt. If this whole 'education slash superintendent slash Texas education policy director' thing doesn't work out, you could walk into any bakery and be confident in your skills."

"You'll write me a reference?" Matt laughed, his mouth full.

"Absolutely." They both laughed, Matt stretching as he stood and reached for his keys and phone. "Are you sure you don't want me to take them with me now?"

"It's okay," Sawyer assured him. "We don't need them sitting in your truck all night. I'll get them there tomorrow by eleven." He paused, wiping down the counter with a wet rag. "You're gonna be there?"

Matt pretended that question didn't make him feel things. "I will be, yeah." Matt chuckled. "I've got the first two-hour shift."

Sawyer grinned. "I'll see you then. Be safe on your way home." Opening the door, he made a little "oof" sound, the air brisk and chilly. "Guess the 'cold' front hit."

Matt gave Sawyer a look, and they both laughed again. "Stay warm," Sawyer told him.

"You too." Matt stepped off the trailer and walked to his truck. "Good night."

· · · · · · · · · · · ·

Matt got to school early the next morning, knowing there'd be a lot of tables and chairs to set up in the parking lot for all the various student clubs. One by one, the student volunteers arrived for their shifts, and he enjoyed spending time with them like this, getting to see them in a different light as they helped set up the tables and booths for the different clubs at school.

True to his word, Sawyer dropped off the cupcakes before the event began, and stayed a few minutes to help set up their table.

"Are you staying, Mr. Evans?" one of the seventh graders asked.

"I can't, Melia," he told her. "I'm meeting up with friends, and we're going to check out a barbecue restaurant in Luling."

No, that didn't bother Matt at all.

The school's Food Fest always had a good turnout, the neighborhood families supportive of the fundraiser. It ran from eleven to three, though Matt only had to stay for the first two hours. Having helped to make the cupcakes, it pleased him to see them selling quickly, everyone excited to try them. Each time someone bought one, he described the flavors as a professional would, speaking with authority on their flavors. The only thing that would've made it better would've been if Sawyer had been there as well. He snapped a picture when the last pumpkin cheesecake cupcake sold and sent it to Sawyer.

"Mateo."

Matt looked up, eyes widening in surprise as his grandparents walked toward him. "Hey." He stepped out from behind the table to greet them. "What are you doing here? Is everything okay?"

"Your grandpa was bored." Elena Navarro leaned in and hugged him tight. "I had to get him out of the house before he started a new 'project,'" she said with air quotes. His grandmother was small in stature, but there was steel in her spine, Matt knew. "So I took him to the tractor supply store to look around."

"You took me?" Hector Navarro stepped up to Matt and gave him a one-armed hug. "How are you doing, *mijo*?" he asked, looking at all the food booths. "*Querida*, do you want anything to eat?" Hector reached for her hand.

"In a minute, *querido*," she replied, giving him a warm smile. "Let's walk around first."

"The coaches are doing burgers, if you guys haven't had lunch." Matt waved at Deanna to let her know he was stepping away for a bit. "The art department's got Frito pies too. But before you leave, come back to my table. I made cupcakes."

They both looked at him, suspicious.

"Okay, I decorated cupcakes. But they're fantastic. I'll save a couple for you two before they're gone."

After his shift, Matt wandered over to the athletics department's table and grabbed a burger and a bag of chips for himself. "Selling a lot?" he asked, handing a five-dollar bill to Bridget Hart, the girls' head coach.

"We'll sell out in an hour," Bridget answered. "I'll admit, I worried about the weather. It's damp and chilly, but the crowds have been busy all day and everyone's been stopping by for lunch before they hit the desserts."

"Speaking of desserts," Paul called out from behind the grill, waving Matt toward him. "I heard you and your friend were making *cupcakes* last night."

"It seems like lots of people have heard that." Matt ignored the pointed look Paul was giving him, the way his voice inflected the word cupcakes. "They're pretty tasty too. You should come buy one and see for yourself."

Paul laughed. "My wife said she bought four of the chocolate ones. She ate two and took two home for me."

Matt reached for his phone after he got into his truck.

Matt: *We're a hit.*

Sawyer: *I'm glad. I had a good time with you last night. Hope you weren't too bored by it all.*

Matt: *I learned a lot from you. If you ever need help baking, let me know.*

Sawyer: *LOL will do.*

November

From: Delores Beck

To: Steven Wong, Cynthia Quinn, Mateo Ruiz, Alicia Mund, Kristine Wood, Coraline Mann, Laverne Sheldon, Tamara Morales, Crystal Moss, Daniel Gotti, Eva Moody

Date: Oct 30

Subject: Potluck farewell

We're having a goodbye party for Sawyer on Friday to celebrate his last day subbing. Dorothy said she might drop by with the baby. Sign-up list on the fridge. Hope everyone can stop by!

– – –

Daisy Beck

Orchestra Director, Sarah Hays Middle School

• • • • • • • • •

A utumn rolled by in the blink of an eye, and before Matt knew it, the first week of November was upon him. He paused by C106 on his way to his classroom, seeing Sawyer setting up worksheets on the front table. "Last day, eh? Glad to be done with this?"

Sawyer grinned, glancing up and catching Matt's eyes. He gave a quiet laugh. "I don't know. I think I was just getting the hang of proportionality."

"Never know when you'll need that." Matt stepped closer into the room. "But for real, you did an outstanding job here. I admit I was kind of a jackass when you arrived, and for that I'm sorry."

"Nah." Sawyer shook his head. "You already had a hectic year scheduled and then got this—" Sawyer pointed at himself, "—flung at you. I needed support and advice, and you saved me." A quiet moment passed, and Sawyer continued. "I appreciate it. You're a great friend...and I'm glad we met."

Matt said nothing, but the silence wasn't unpleasant. He punched the door frame lightly with his fist. "I'll catch you at lunch."

"Will do," Sawyer replied, turning back to the papers on his desk.

Matt walked into the lunchroom the same time as the early lunch group was taking off, but there was still plenty of food on the counter. Sawyer and the others were throwing away their paper plates and grabbing cookies and brownies for the road as the bell rang. "Quite the shindig," Matt said, admiring the spread. "Daisy made brownies. She only does that for special occasions."

"We needed to make sure Sawyer knew we appreciated him." Daisy wrapped a napkin around a plate of snacks. "Also, I'm having dental surgery next month and I'll be out for two days." She smirked. "I want him to take up my sub job."

"Already got you penciled in the calendar," Sawyer said with a wink, "so the bribe was appreciated but unnecessary." He walked out the door with one last look back at Matt, who somehow was already looking forward to Sawyer coming back to campus and subbing for other teachers.

This wasn't goodbye, not really, and while that didn't exactly make him happy, it lessened the sadness in an awkward and indescribable way.

· · · · ·· · · · ·

Monday morning, Matt waved at Terrence Mendez, their assistant principal, as he walked into the building. He jogged upstairs and turned into the C hallway and stopped.

The light was on in C106.

Matt poked his head in, half expecting to see that now-familiar lanky frame, the golden hair pulled into a ponytail. But no, it was a familiar woman standing at the white board, her back turned away from the door as she composed the day's agenda. "Welcome back, Dorothy." He stepped into the room. "How are you doing?" he asked, sitting on top of a student desk.

"You know, I'm sort of glad to be back at work." Dorothy leaned against the board, then dropped her head with a laugh. "Who am I kidding? I wish I were home." She reached for her phone and showed Matt a few pictures of her newborn daughter, the spitting image of her mother with a pile of black hair and a wide smile. "Cora said the sub did a remarkable job. Thanks for supporting him. I know you have a lot going on in your life right now."

"It was my pleasure." Matt wasn't surprised how much he meant it. "And after a couple of weeks, he took on most of the work. Kids seemed to like him too."

"I hear they're an interesting group this year," she said, and they spent a few minutes getting caught up on the scope and sequence and light workplace gossip. "Thanks again for helping us out. I owe you one, Matt."

· · · · ● · ● · · · ·

The next few weeks unsettled Matt, and he never felt like he was quite in the groove. Some days he expected to see Sawyer around every corner, disappointed when he wasn't there. Other times, it caught Matt off guard when he'd spot Sawyer walking down a different hallway or see him on the other side of school. This indescribable spark of joy would quietly explode inside him, even if they didn't speak. Sure, he could call Sawyer and invite him out for a friendly beer, or just text to see how he was doing, but he never did.

It was stupid, this crush of his, but it was harmless. Matt knew it wasn't going anywhere, and yet somehow, just knowing Sawyer might be there was enough.

· · · · ● · ● · · · ·

The days before a major holiday always felt electrified, and the week of Thanksgiving was no exception. Students and staff had a two-day school week, with Wednesday through Friday off. Attendance was often poor that week, many students pulled out of school on Monday and Tuesday ahead of the holiday so families could get started on their travels.

"Is it me, or are the kids even more off the wall today?" Cora asked, waiting behind Matt at the copy machine before school on Tuesday before the holiday break. She held up a copy of a word search in the shape of a turkey. "This is as much as I'm hoping for today. How are yours doing?"

Matt shrugged. "Meh. I booked the computer lab, so they're playing an online game to review, and the kids are having fun. But there's not much for me to do. I've been catching up on emails and harassing kids for missing work if they're here."

"I admire your dedication." Cora leaned against the counter and exhaled. "I'm ready to get out of here for a couple of days. Do you have plans for the holiday?"

"Just the ranch. Sabrina called on Sunday and asked if I could come tomorrow and help with fence repair." Finishing one print job for the algebra class, he changed the master copies and began running another set for his eighth graders, getting things ready for the following week. "Apparently a couple cows got loose last week and ended up on the highway." That had been quite the phone call from his grandmother. "How 'bout you?"

"The plan is to go to Dallas. We'll see how the weather holds. They're forecasting storms up there." Cora looked at Matt for a moment, then continued. "Have you talked to Sawyer recently?"

"I haven't," Matt answered, hiding his disappointment about that. "I texted him the other day about basketball tryouts. He'd mentioned he wanted to see a game when we started playing, but I haven't heard from him or anything."

Cora grinned. "He's a great guy."

"Yeah, I know." Matt anticipated where this conversation was going. His print job couldn't end fast enough; all he wanted to do was get out of this room.

"Matt. He's a great guy," she repeated.

He rubbed his forehead. "What are you doing?" he asked, turning and facing her.

Her face filled with a cheerful smile. "You two liked each other." The look on his face made her smile falter. "And there's nothing wrong with that."

"I don't have time for dating right now." Matt gathered up all his copies. "You know that."

Then he felt an arm around him, Cora giving him a hug. "We all love you, and want you to be happy. Seems a shame to let an opportunity pass you by. And," she added, setting her paper on top of the copy machine tray, "he's away from his family right now. I'm thinking he might be a little lonely too."

· · · · ● · ● · · · ·

Matt always looked forward to Thanksgiving break, but this year more than the past. He'd put off writing an annotated bibliography for his Research Methods class and planned on spending a couple of days focused on that while staying at the ranch, maybe even getting ahead in the readings in his other class. Thanksgiving itself he could take or leave. It'd never been one of Matt's favorite holidays; their family was small, and they seldom traveled because of the animals at the ranch. The situation with his mother sometimes made his grandma sad at the holidays, but he appreciated the time off from work.

His grandmother's side dishes weren't bad, either.

Wednesday morning, Matt packed a bag with warm clothes and his laptop and headed out. Fog had rolled in early, and the day threatened to be one of those damp, chilly days, but Matt knew the fence needed to be fixed, and the sooner, the better. It was about forty-five minutes from Matt's front door to the road turning off the highway toward the ranch. Half a mile down on the right of that paved road was the entrance to Rancho Rio Riendo, three Rs emblazoned on the large metal gate. Matt stopped his truck, opening the gate and driving through, closing the gate behind him.

He turned onto a dirt road, driving past a pasture with about thirty cows grazing lazily, pulling up to a one-story ranch-style house with a wide fenced-in yard. Several giant oaks shaded the path to the front door. To the left of the house was an old barn, its broad wooden door open, and two black labs ran out, speeding toward Matt's pickup as they spotted him pulling up to the house.

He parked in his usual spot under the carport. Matt saw his grandfather tending to his garden out back and waved as he stepped out of his truck. "Hi, Grandpa." He hefted his bag over his shoulder and strolled toward the older man. The dogs, Pancho and Lefty, danced around him, excited.

Hector Navarro stood up and stretched when his grandson walking toward him. "Mateo, good to see you. I thought you'd be here tomorrow." He opened the back gate, holding it open. Glancing over at Matt's old truck, he chuckled. "When are you going to get rid of that and get something new? It's almost as old as you are." Hector snorted, running a hand through his graying hair. "It wasn't even a new truck when I bought it."

Matt shook his head adamantly. "I'm driving it until the wheels fall off."

"That won't be long now," Hector said as they stepped into the backyard, the dogs following them. He picked up the basket of vegetables he'd collected that morning and led Matt through the backyard and back door of the house and into the kitchen. He set the basket on the counter as they stepped into the living room. "Elena, look who's here?"

"I'm back here," a female voice called out from the back of the house. "I'm coming." Matt's grandmother popped out of the guest room that served as her computer room and sewing room. "Hi, *mijo*," she said, embracing him in a tight hug. "Sabrina said you were on your way. Thanks for helping her with the fence. I told her we could hire someone to come fix it, but..." Elena shrugged, exasperated. "She's determined to take care of it herself. Well, with a little help from you and Grandpa."

"We'll get it done." Hector gave Matt a shoulder squeeze. "And your computer, *querida*, ask him about that."

Elena turned back to Matt. "My printer isn't working. Will you look at it" she asked, a hopeful look in her eyes.

"Tech support has arrived." Matt touched an invisible hat on his head and kissed her cheek. "I'll look after we get done with the fence."

Matt unpacked the clothes he'd brought with him and set his laptop on his desk. He enjoyed having a sizable room all to himself out here at the ranch. When his grandparents had built this house, he suspected they must've expected a peaceful retirement, living out their days on the land they loved, working it until they couldn't anymore and spending time together after a life of raising not just their child, but their daughter's children.

Could they have imagined that neither of those grandchildren would ever move out? Or maybe they had, because all the bedrooms were spacious, accommodating their grown-up needs. He'd never lived here as a child, so there was no sentimental attachment, but just the same, the room was his and suited him perfectly.

He changed into old jeans and a sweatshirt and walked toward the barn to find his little sister. Sure enough, she was loading rolls of barbed wire onto a light utility trailer hitched to a four-wheeler. "What did they do back in the day when they rode horses out to fix the fences?" He grinned, leaning in for a hug.

Sabrina snorted. She'd pulled her long, black hair into a ponytail, tucked under a Texas A&M baseball cap. "I guess some poor schmuck got to carry all that out there." She pointed at a pile of metal T-posts leaning against an empty stable door. "Can you put those in the trailer?"

Matt helped her gather all the tools they'd need and found a pair of work gloves in one of the tool chests. Soon they each climbed on an ATV, and Matt followed Sabrina out toward the property line.

"So, how are things going, sis?" he asked as they took down the temporary fencing she'd set up after the cows escaped. "You okay?"

"Oh, yeah. Everyone's doing good. But there's always something to fix." She looked down the fence line, walking toward one of the wooden posts. "We should replace these soon. Not today," she added, "but they didn't update this stretch the last time they put in new fencing."

"That'll be expensive." Matt pounded the T-posts into the ground wherever Sabrina pointed. "How are things going here? They doing okay?"

She laughed. "They're great. I swear, I think they're friskier with each other now than when they were our age."

Not the mental image Matt wanted, but he enjoyed hearing they were still very much in love. "And you? What happened with that guy you were texting with?"

Her face darkened. "Turns out he jumped the gun a little when he said his divorce was final."

Oh, shit. "You alright?"

"Me? Yeah, always." Sabrina wiped sweat off her face. "Besides, I got plenty to keep me busy here. What about you? Anyone special in your life?"

Matt scoffed and changed the subject. "How's the ranch doing?"

"We break even," Sabrina said. "Grandpa talks about bringing in more cows, but something always gets in the way. I think he knows he can't help as much as he used to, and he doesn't like the idea of hiring help."

"There used to be workers here all the time."

"I'm not saying it makes sense." Sabrina looked back over at the pasture where the cows stood, watching them. "But calves are a lot of work, and I really don't want to look after a bigger herd than we've got now." She shrugged, giving him a small smile. "So, we'll see." She held the wire stretcher while Matt stapled them into the wooden posts.

They repeated the process until they'd replaced all the broken fencing. Matt tugged the fence, testing its stability. "That oughta hold the girls in," he murmured, pleased with his work. "There's nothing on the other side of that fence they could want."

"Oh, Matt." Sabrina sighed, placing their tools back onto the trailer. "Bless your heart, it's a good thing you're gay, 'cause you don't know shit about women."

· · · · ●· ● · · ·

His hot shower felt amazing that night, Matt standing under the steamy water for much longer than usual. Despite his daily exercise routine, Matt had used muscles today that weren't often worked. He was sore, but in the best way, aching from a day of hard work. After dinner, he went to his room to work on his paper. Two hours later, Matt turned off his computer and lay down on his bed.

He wasn't sleepy, not yet, so he picked up his phone and opened a dating app he looked at when he was bored, or curious...or horny. Changing his location to Houston, Matt scrolled from one man to another, swiping occasionally to the right when he spotted someone attractive. But tonight, no one caught his eye, and even though a couple of guys texted him back right away, that spark of excitement wasn't there.

Ron (27, Conroe) had enough shirtless pics on his profile that Matt worried for a second that he might not own any.

BJ (24, Sugar Land) texted immediately after Matt swiped right, asking if Matt wanted to meet. Definite turn-off, at least tonight.

Mark (37, Katy) was older than Matt, but fuck... Matt was going to be thirty this year. Maybe this was his future, hooking up with older guys. Then it hit him—soon he'd be the older guy on this app. Fuck.

A couple of times his cock twitched with interest, but nobody who made him stop and take notice.

Or perhaps his thoughts were with someone else tonight.

It didn't take Matt long to realize he'd been comparing all the men in the app to Sawyer and how he made Matt feel. He closed the app and put the phone down next to him on the bed. Turning on the television, he flipped channels for a while, but nothing held his attention. Frustrated, he walked out of his bedroom and ambled to the kitchen. He stopped by the fridge and pulled out one of Sabrina's hard ciders. He felt restless in his skin and didn't know how to shake it.

Back in his room, Matt flopped onto his bed again, then sat back up. Taking a sip from the cider, Matt stared at the app one more time before sliding it closed for good, opening his messaging app. His fingers seemed to fly of their own accord. *How's your week been?*

Matt set his phone down. It vibrated a few minutes later.

> Sawyer: *Not too bad. 2nd grade at the elementary school yesterday and today. I'm hanging out with the dog tonight. Was thinking about going camping for a couple of days since school is out.*

Not traveling back home to visit his family. Interesting. Matt pressed on.

> Matt: *Doing anything for Thanksgiving?*
> Sawyer: *Miss Amanda was doing a turkey for the trailer folk lol. I offered to help, but that's Her Thing, I*

guess.

Matt: You wanna come have thanksgiving with us?
You could camp out here on our land if you wanted,
or stay in the guest room.

Matt stared at his message for a long moment before hitting send. This wasn't about hitting on a cute guy; this was about a friend. His friend.

There was a protracted pause before Sawyer answered, three little dots that meant he was responding. It seemed like forever before the words appeared.

Sawyer: You sure?

Sawyer had typed and erased something; there should've been more there.

Matt: Yeah, it'll be fun. You can ask my grandma
about some of her recipes if you were interested in
authentic Tex-Mex food.
Sawyer: Wow that would be amazing. Are you really
sure?
Matt: Yeah. Bring the dog, stay for a couple of days.
We're eating around one, but you can get here as
early as you want.

There was another extended pause before Sawyer responded.

Sawyer: I'll let you know when I leave. Thanks again,
M.

He sent Sawyer directions to the ranch. Still not sure what'd just happened, Matt lay down and stared at the ceiling. They were friends; he was being nice to a friend.

That was all, he told himself, smiling as he fell asleep.

· · · · ● · ● · · ·

Matt padded barefoot into the kitchen the next morning, unsurprised to see his grandparents already up and running around. "Morning," he said, yawning as Elena slid over his University of Texas mug filled with coffee, made the way he liked it. Matt spotted his grandfather dragging a large box of peanut oil from the pantry. "Let me help you with that, okay?"

"Finish your coffee first," Hector answered. "But it needs to go outside on the porch, *por favor.*"

"Will do." Matt paused a moment, then continued. "Hey, um, I was hoping it'd be okay if I invited a colleague over for lunch today. He's from out of state and doesn't have any family here."

A quick glance passed between them, and Elena smiled. "Of course, *mijo,* that's fine. The more, the merrier."

"You know your grandma always makes too much food anyway," Hector teased.

"Says the man who's frying two turkeys for four people." She looked over at Matt, curious. "Is he staying the night?"

Matt nodded. "Um, I told him we had room here if he wanted to. He also mentioned he felt like camping, so we might go out and camp by the riverfront if it doesn't rain." Matt paused. "We don't have any hunters this weekend, do we?"

"Not for the holiday weekend," Hector said. "I think the weather's going to hold. It'll be a pleasant night for being outside," he added, gathering the rest of his tools before stepping outside.

Later that morning, Matt was helping his grandfather set up the fryer out on the back patio when he spotted a dark blue truck driving up the road, the dogs running toward the fence line, barking as the truck approached.

"Your friend is here," Hector told him, and Matt tried to push those butterflies in his stomach down.

He crossed the yard and opened the backyard gate and walked over to the carport. Matt saw Sawyer pull up behind his truck. "You found it."

"I did." Sawyer grinned, stepping out of the driver's side of his truck. He walked over to the passenger side, opened the door, and grabbed his backpack. "I wasn't sure how serious you were about the camping, but I brought a tent and my camp stove." Sawyer pointed to the backseat of his truck. "Oh, and this—" Sawyer reached in and pulled out a clear plastic pie carrier. "I made a dessert." He glanced over Matt's shoulder. "No nut allergies, I hope. I should've asked."

Matt turned his head and spotted his grandfather approaching. "No nut allergies." Matt turned to look at his grandfather. "Grandpa, this is my friend, Sawyer Evans. Sawyer, this is my grandfather, Hector Navarro."

"Pleased to meet you, sir." Sawyer extended his hand. "Thank you for letting me impose on your family this holiday."

"Any friend of Mateo's is *familia* to us. We're glad you can join us." Hector shook his hand, and his eyes lingered a few minutes over Sawyer's truck. "Ram 3500?" he asked. "2014?"

"2013," Sawyer answered. "I travel a lot and pull an Airstream, so it's got the tow package."

Hector whistled low and patted the front hood several times, admiration in his eyes. "This is what you need, Mateo. Come on, boys, let's go inside."

Sawyer reached into his truck and pulled out a small crate. Matt saw Biscuit's sad face peering out. "Matt said the dogs are friendly?"

"All bark and no bite. They're terrible watch dogs—everyone's their friend," Hector assured him as they strolled into the backyard, closing the gate behind them.

Sawyer set the crate down and opened it up. It took a moment, but soon Biscuit stepped outside, sniffed the other dogs, and then ran for the far end of the yard, the other two dogs following her, tails wagging playfully.

Matt and Sawyer followed Hector, making their way through the backyard, past the garden and inside the back door into the kitchen. "Elena, we've got company."

Elena came out from around the corner, a bright smile on her face as she wiped her hands on her oversized apron. "Hello," she said, arms extended as she gave Sawyer a hug. "Welcome to *el rancho*."

"Thank you. I know I've only seen the yard and the kitchen, but this is gorgeous. The drive out here was so peaceful."

Elena beamed with pride. "It's our little piece of heaven." Elena noticed Matt was carrying a pie container. "Mateo, what's that?"

Sawyer grinned. "I made a chocolate pecan pie. I hope that's okay." He glanced over as Matt set it down on the kitchen island and lifted the cover. "I like to cook."

Elena's face broke into a wide smile. "That's better than okay, that's marvelous," she said, reaching over and slapping Hector's hand as he broke off a piece of the crust. "*Deja de hacer eso,*" she muttered at him, shaking her head. "Mateo, go show Sawyer where the guest room is while I get after your grandpa."

"Yes, ma'am." Matt nudged Sawyer to follow him and led him through the living room and down the hall, pointing out the bathroom, the laundry room, and the guest room along the way. "My sister Sabrina ran into town. That's her room." Matt pointed at the end of the hallway. "And I'm across the hall."

Sawyer dropped his bag on the bed, looking around.

"My grandma uses this for her projects. Sewing, her computer, stuff like that." Matt pointed to a quilt thrown over a computer. "Does Biscuit want to sleep inside with you or out on the porch with the others?"

Sawyer laughed. "I guess we'll see. She doesn't have much opportunity for company." Pulling a curtain aside, Matt saw the three dogs all chasing each other around the large yard, stopping every few minutes to smell something new on the ground before starting up again. "She'll be tired tonight, that's for certain."

"Definitely," Matt agreed. "Okay, you get settled. I'm going to go help my grandpa set up the turkey fryer. We only use it once a year and we have to remember how to put it together each year. You're welcome to join us—"

"Yeah, of course." Sawyer answered at once. "Sounds like fun. Let's go." He followed Matt out of the room. But as they traveled through the kitchen, they spotted Elena in front of the sink, washing her hands. "Can I help you with anything?" Sawyer asked.

"No, you're our guest," Elena told him. "Mateo said you worked with him at his school. I know you all need to rest and relax during these breaks."

"I substitute at Matt's school, yes, but I wasn't kidding when I said I liked to cook. Back in Portland, where I'm from, I, um, co-owned a restaurant." Elena looked over at Matt for confirmation. "I worked in the kitchen with them all the time."

"Don't let him fool you." Matt looked over at Sawyer before turning back to his grandmother. "He was the executive chef for a successful restaurant." Sawyer looked up and caught Matt's eyes, the two of them staring at each other for what seemed like a long moment.

Elena watched them, smiling before she spoke. "You want to chop some onions?" She set Sawyer up on the kitchen island at his own prep station, where he began quickly mincing onions into neat little piles. Matt gave him a brief salute and stepped outside to join his grandfather.

Sawyer opened up a little more over Thanksgiving lunch. "The restaurant was called Scordatura. It's a music term. My partner was a music nerd." He paused, lost in a memory for a moment. "It's still there, at least it was last time I checked. I loved it—the cooking part I mean. Overseeing menus, working in the kitchens with the brigade. But my business partner wanted out, so we sold."

"You ever thought about opening another restaurant?" Sabrina asked, digging into her turkey and mashed potatoes. "Estella is in dire need of a fine dining establishment or two."

Sawyer took a bite of his turkey and dressing, chewing slowly before he answered. "It's hard work, and most restaurants fail. I'm not sure I'm up for that again, and I couldn't do it alone. I like the cooking part, but the business stuff, that's where I'm weak. So right now, I'm enjoying the travel, picking up new ideas and recipes, and making my videos."

"You should write a cookbook." Elena looked over at Sawyer and Matt. "Mateo said you make videos, but there are some of us who still buy cookbooks."

"That's an idea," Sawyer answered. "I know there's so many cooking techniques to learn here in Texas, so I imagine I'll be here a while picking up the culture and the cuisine."

Sabrina chuckled. "The man wants cuisine, and we fry him a turkey."

Everyone joined in the joke, but Sawyer shook his head. "But for real, this turkey is incredible. Never had a fried turkey before."

"The secret is the brining," Hector told them. "And the peanut oil."

After lunch, Matt sliced the pie, sliding thick wedges onto small plates and passing them out.

Elena sighed, digging into her piece. "This is so good. You're going to share the recipe with me, yes?"

"Perhaps we can work out some mutual recipe sharing," Sawyer said with a grin. "Do you make your own enchilada sauce?"

"Of course." Elena leaned over, and soon they began discussing the finer points of chili powder. Matt grinned as he observed them.

"He's nice," Sabrina said in a hushed voice.

Matt nodded. "Yeah. I'm glad he's not alone for the holiday." When Sabrina didn't answer, Matt glanced over at her, disconcerted by the way she stared at him. "What?"

"Nothing, brother," she answered. "Just glad to know that you've got...friends."

Sabrina set herself in charge of cleanup. Hector went to take a nap, and Elena sat on the sofa and watched television while Matt and Sawyer took apart the turkey fryer.

"Thanks again for inviting me," Sawyer said. "That meal was incredible. Your grandparents are wonderful people. I can understand why you come out here so often."

Matt looked around, seeing the ranch with fresh eyes. "It was a great place to grow up." He paused, then added, "I'm glad you came."

Sawyer's smile was blinding. "Me too."

Later that afternoon, Matt found Sawyer outside in the backyard, playing with the dogs. "Did you want to go camping tonight? We can stay out for a day or two, or only an overnighter, depending on how much time you've got." He stopped, realizing Sawyer hadn't invited him to camp with him, not in so many words. "I mean," he began, "I'm up for it if you want company. If you want to be alone, that's cool. I like to go out there sometimes on my own and be by myself, listening to the river and the animals. You won't hurt my feelings if you'd rather be alone."

"No." Sawyer shook his head. "I'm not looking for solitude." That bright smile lit up Sawyer's face, their gaze holding for a second too long. "Come with me."

"Yeah," Matt answered without thinking. "That's good. Sounds like a plan. We can get some food and other stuff to take out there."

Sawyer grinned. "I'll grab my things."

Thirty minutes later, they were packed and ready. Matt loaded a bag with leftovers and a few bottles of beer into a cooler and placed it into the bed of Sawyer's truck, along with a couple of folding camp chairs and a stack of firewood.

Sawyer sat on the porch, petting his dog. "You be a good girl, okay? You hear me? I don't want a bad report from Miss Elena."

Sabrina laughed, calling the small dog over to her lap, scratching her behind the ears. "She'll be fine. You guys have fun," she called out as they climbed into the truck.

Sawyer started the engine. "How far are we going?" he asked, backing the truck up and driving down a well-worn dirt path behind the barn.

"Close to a mile," Matt said. "Not that far, but this way we don't have to lug everything, and we can drive back quick if we need to use the bathroom or something."

Sawyer laughed. "We're really roughing it."

"I don't know about you, but I had a big lunch." Matt snorted at his own joke. "But I've got a roll of toilet paper and a shovel in case shitting in the woods feels more authentic to you."

Sawyer groaned. "I'll see how I feel when the time comes." They drove past the barn and onto a less traveled but still visible path. "How much of this does your family own?"

"It's a little under three hundred acres." Matt pointed in the direction where he wanted Sawyer to go as the path ended. "Used to be more, but my grandpa sold some of it when they built the house and started cutting back on the ranch work. Their retirement fund, I guess. It's a strange shape, more like a fat letter L than a square or rectangle. We've got over half a mile of the riverfront. There, that's a good spot." Matt indicated a flat area underneath a large oak tree close to the river. "I've camped out here before."

Sawyer turned off the truck, and they got out, looking around at the level ground. Sawyer wandered toward the water's edge. "This is gorgeous. How long has this land been in your family?" They pulled things out of the back of the truck and set up their small camp. "Did your grandparents buy it?"

"Oh, no." Matt looked around proudly at the land. "It's been in the family for a while. My grandma grew up here. I think it was her dad who bought the land way back when. There was more land back then, and it's whittled down through the years."

Sawyer swept rocks off the ground, spreading a tarp before he set up his small tent. He looked over at Matt, watching him curiously. "Did you bring a tent of your own, or are you gonna sleep right under the stars, like some wild animal?"

Matt threw him a dirty look. "I brought blankets and a pillow. I thought I'd just sleep back here." He tapped on the truck bed. "It's not that cold out tonight. That'll be enough." He looked up at the sun settling in the west. "Better get set up. It'll be dark soon."

Matt put the campfire together while Sawyer fixed his tent. It wasn't cold, but to Matt, it didn't feel like proper camping without a fire. It was getting dark, and he saw the stars coming out one by one. "I used to come out here when I was younger, sleep on the ground and look out at the night sky," he said, setting the camp chairs around the fire, pulling out two bottles of beer.

"That sounds so cool. Is that why you wanted to go into aerospace?" Sawyer accepted his beer and settled down in his chair with a satisfied sound. "Growing up looking at the stars?"

Matt took a long swig before answering. How to describe what he felt when he looked at the night sky. "Not really, but yes." He shook his head. "I mean, when I was a kid, I remember watching Pathfinder land, reading all about it. Later, when I was in high school, they launched the Mars rovers." Matt laughed to himself. "I followed those missions like some kind of groupie. Posters on my walls and everything."

"What a weirdo." Sawyer answered with a teasing fondness in his voice. "I love it."

Matt picked up a small stone and threw it at Sawyer. "I liked robotics, the way those little machines obeyed their commands and protocol. Doing their job, day in and day out. And...there was something about the idea of working on a machine that would touch another planet—it seemed so unattainable, all I wanted was to be a part of that happening." Matt looked up and Sawyer was staring at him. "What?"

"You just..." Sawyer hesitated, looking for the right words. "You sound so passionate about it."

"I was." He took another swig from his beer. "So how long do you think you'll be here? Texas, I mean?"

Sawyer shook his head. "Not sure. I thought I might spend a year in the state, and I got here in...January, I think. I was in El Paso a while, then worked at a ranch in Marfa for a month. There's a lot to pick up here—I mean, so many kinds of food and culture. But I've been in Estella for four months already. Wasn't planning on being here this long."

Matt didn't like that answer, but it wasn't unexpected. "Ever think about heading home and trying the restaurant business again?"

"Honestly, I couldn't go it alone. Maybe one day." Sawyer played with the loose paper wrapper on his beer bottle. "But right now, this is enough for me. I enjoy traveling and meeting people and learning about food. This autumn, I've had a lot of fun with the kids, if that makes sense. Subbing is fun when I've parked myself in one place for a few months. But one day, when I'm ready, I'm sure I'll put my food knowledge to good use and cook professionally again." He smiled. "It's what I was born to do."

Maybe Matt imagined it, but he felt a slight personal dig, coupled with Sawyer's earlier comment about Matt's passion about his former dreams. He pushed that aside. "Your family couldn't help you?"

Sawyer looked at the fire for a long minute before turning his face up toward Matt. "It's not that they couldn't help me. They're not entirely pleased with the choices I'm making in my life right now. Dad's a lawyer, brother is a lawyer, and Sawyer is a cook."

"You weren't a cook," Matt told him.

"Tell that to my parents. I took all the law school money my grandparents left me and bought a restaurant. A successful one, but even that wasn't enough for them to forgive me." Sawyer drank a sip from his beer. "And then I sold said successful restaurant and bought a camper. Went hippie, which was more than their blessed liberal hearts could handle. It was like, 'Sawyer, we can forgive the gay. That's okay, but did you want to be a pauper too?'"

Hearing that shocked Matt. "That's kind of hurtful."

"Yes, it was." Sawyer took another swig from his drink. "My lack of ambition is an affront to them. My interpretation of what is successful isn't the same as theirs."

"Do you talk to them often?"

"Not that often."

Matt never let a day go by without speaking to his grandmother. "Sorry to hear about that, man."

"Some families are like that. What about you?" Sawyer asked. "Sabrina said she hadn't spoken to your mom in years. I didn't —" He paused. "I guess I didn't realize she was still alive."

"Not that it matters," Matt muttered, then shook his head. "I'm sorry, that was flippant, and you asked a serious question."

Sawyer took a swig from his beer. "Well, your answer explains a lot."

Matt looked at the fire. "She left us, and I don't think about her at all."

"And Sabrina?"

"She doesn't remember her much. She was little when our mother left, just a baby."

Sawyer smiled sadly. "So that's why your grandparents raised you."

"Yeah." Matt nodded. "They're the best people I know. Imagine working hard your entire life, raising your kid, and as soon as she's grown and you've made it to that time in your lives when you should plan fun trips, retiring to the ranch and enjoying your life, boom. Two little kids get dropped on your doorstep, and you get to raise a family all over again." Matt could never repay them.

"They love you two so much."

"They do," Matt agreed, "but it's been hard on them, I know."

Sawyer stretched out his legs in front of him. "I keep meaning to ask you. What is that name they call each other? I tried looking it up, but I don't think I'm close to spelling it right."

Matt grinned. "*Querido*. Or *querida*, depending on who's talking. It means 'my dear' and 'sweetheart,' something like that.

Fifty years together, and they still can't stay away from each other."

"We should all be so lucky." Sawyer had a sad expression on his face as he looked at the fire.

Matt finished his beer, tossing the bottle on the ground next to the cooler. "So, Mister World Traveler," he began, changing the subject. "Tell me about all the places you and your trailer have been."

"Not traveling the world, not exactly," Sawyer said. He started talking about his favorite travel spots: the red rocks of Moab, Utah; the Redwoods in California; the cold beaches of Washington. "There was this one spot—here, I think I still have the picture." He handed Matt his phone, leaning over and scrolling over several images until he stopped at one of Sawyer holding up an enormous salmon. But Sawyer scrolled one photo too far, and Matt saw what looked to be a selfie of Sawyer, shirtless and in front of a mirror—a picture he'd shared with others, he guessed. Matt saw those arm tattoos went all the way up Sawyer's shoulders, with another on the left side of his torso. "Oops." Sawyer closed the photograph quickly. Even in the firelight, Matt saw him flush. "Sorry 'bout that."

"Don't worry about it," Matt told him, as if he wasn't committing it to memory. It made him curious about who Sawyer spent his free time with, and what had happened before he'd come to Texas. Before he'd come into Matt's life. "So, your restaurant. Your partner. What happened there?"

It was a few seconds before Sawyer answered. "The lesson learned there was that you shouldn't mix business with pleasure." Leaning back in his chair, he continued. "I'll say he broke my heart. He'd tell you I broke his. I was young and dumb and not ready to be anyone's business partner." They were quiet for several minutes, both men just enjoying being outside, surrounded by nature. The sounds of the river and the animals in the distance, the smells of the campfire. "Can I ask you a personal question?"

"Yeah, sure." Matt picked up a long stick and poked at the fire. "Fuck knows I've asked enough of you tonight."

Sawyer chuckled low. "We're sharing all over the place, I guess. Anyway, I'm curious. What's your story?" he asked, leaning forward and staring at Matt with a soft expression on his face. "You seem to have done things the right way. Clearly a family man, raised right by good people. How come you haven't brought a nice Hispanic boy home to Elena, settled down with a white picket fence, and popped out a couple of kids? Lack of opportunity, or are you just one of those super-picky gays?"

"Yes and...yes, I guess?" Matt stared at the fire, then back up at Sawyer. "The people here in town, they're not as awful as they could be. At least not to my face. I guess it helps that I grew up here, and a lot of these people have known me all my life, so I'm not dangerous, not waving my gay agenda in their faces. And," he added, "my grandparents are fantastic people, respected in the community. I haven't had that many people being outright assholes to me about being gay. At least not to my face."

Yeah, there had been those times when he'd been younger, teased; pointed looks and sharp comments that had slipped through his thick skin and pierced him.

"I'm not opposed to the idea of being in a relationship, but when would I have time for that right now? And..." Matt hesitated, trying to figure out his words. "I think once I'm an admin, or in some position of authority, it'd be harder for anyone to give me grief about being a fag."

Sawyer watched Matt as he spoke, those wide blue eyes searching for something. It felt intrusive. "Do you think they'd harass you about that right now?"

Matt shrugged. "I'm the gay teacher. At least, the only one at the school who'll admit to it, because c'mon, April, your roommate is not just your 'roommate' and we all know it. Worst-kept secret in the school. But even then, no one talks about it. I mean, the coaches, they don't give me shit about it, sometimes teasing me a little but nothing that's ever felt mean-spirited. The admin pretends it's not an issue."

"It shouldn't be an issue," Sawyer told him, his voice quiet and low.

"The parents, I don't know, I haven't gotten too many comments since I've been here, and I credit that to being... discreet."

Sawyer's brows raised. "You don't rub their faces in your queerness?"

"Something like that."

Sawyer got quiet again. "What do you do for fun?"

"I go to Austin," Matt said. "Sometimes Houston. Meet up with old friends, an occasional hookup in a big city when I want to get laid."

"Sounds lonely."

Matt snorted. "Says the man who travels in an RV across the country with his dog."

Sawyer blinked and then laughed at that, a quiet sound. "And there we are." Reaching out, he lifted his bottle of beer. "Happy Thanksgiving, Matt."

"Back at you." Matt took a long swig and finished his beer. Sawyer had become a friend, one Matt would never embarrass with his silly romantic longings. "Thanks for coming over."

"Anytime." Sawyer leaned back and looking up at the star-filled sky so intently that Matt glanced up as well. "Anytime."

Matt woke up the next morning to birdsong, dawn breaking. His back ached from sleeping in the bed of Sawyer's truck, but he could only blame himself, pretending to be a tough badass who didn't need a mattress. He sat up and looked around, noticing Sawyer's tent flap was already open.

There he was, standing close to the river, camera in hand. Looking farther past Sawyer's line of sight, Matt spotted two deer about twenty yards ahead, drinking from the water. The morning light through the oak trees made the water sparkle, and Matt fell in love with the land again, through Sawyer's eyes.

Once Sawyer returned to the campsite, they warmed up Thanksgiving leftovers on the camp stove and had a quick breakfast. "How long would it take to walk around the property?" Sawyer asked.

Matt grinned. "A couple of hours, not too long. I'll give you a tour." They walked out first toward the rear of the property. Oak and mesquite trees covered most of the land, with small shrubs and tall grass growing in spots where the sun peeked through the tree canopies. "See that over there?" Matt pointed at a deer blind at the top of a hill. "My grandparents lease this part of the property to hunters during hunting season, people from town they know. They come out and hunt for a day or two. Deer mostly, but we might spot a turkey." They walked past a deer feeder and Matt explained how it worked, spreading the corn around the ground in the morning and evening.

"Grandma feeds them when they come close to the house. It pisses my grandpa off, because they get into his garden."

"They're both amazing people." Sawyer stepped carefully as they walked, as if hoping to see more of the wildlife, trying to coax it to come out.

They made it to the back fence line, and Matt began leading them over toward the pastures in the front. "It used to be a real serious cattle ranch when my great grandfather ran it. They raised beef cattle and shipped them up to northern markets. My grandpa kept that up for a while. I remember, when I was little, it was more of a cow and calf operation, several hundred head."

"What happened?" Sawyer asked as the trees gave way to grass.

"He got older. He had workers to help him, but..." Matt paused a moment as they approached a wide gate leading into a grassy pasture, opening it so they could walk through. "They had a son, but he died when he was little. He's buried over there." Matt pointed to a group of trees behind the main house. "My mom was their only other child, and she didn't like the ranch. At least, she didn't want to live here." Matt had no doubts she'd have liked the money she could get from selling the place. "Grandpa sold most of the cattle off as time passed, and now they just live out here, tending the land. I think he rents out the far pasture sometimes to other ranchers."

They walked toward a large pond, and Matt pointed out the fresh hoof-prints in the mud. "This is so cool." Sawyer's eyes lit up, looking everywhere as he drank it all in, taking pictures here and there. "I'm not sure I would ever leave."

"It's beautiful, but it's a lot of work." Matt spotted a group of cows lying down under a large cedar tree and pointed them out to Sawyer, who snapped a couple of pictures, including one of Matt.

"Don't you think what you're doing now is a lot of work too?"

Matt laughed. "I mean, yeah, but it's different. I don't know how to explain it."

"Do you ever regret not getting back into engineering?" Sawyer asked.

Matt wasn't sure why Sawyer brought up the previous night's conversation. Some words were easier to share in the dark, in front of a fire and under a blanket of stars, not in the cold light of day. "No. I made a decision, and I will not second guess it now because things didn't turn out the way I wanted them to. I don't know if I believe in fate, or God, but I can't imagine there's a divine hand out there that gave my grandma cancer, so I'd change my major and stay closer to home. Shit happens, and we deal with it the best way we can."

"You're an optimist." Sawyer looked like he didn't quite believe that, even though those were his words.

"I'm a realist," Matt answered. "Look around. I have a great life, Sawyer. I refuse to cry because I didn't get to design a Mars rover." At least, not anymore. "Was I upset when it happened? Yeah. I'm not saying it didn't hurt, giving up on a 'dream,'" he added, the last word in air quotes.

"I think it's okay to admit disappointment." Sawyer was watching Matt carefully as he spoke. "It's not a personal failing when your dreams don't come true."

"I didn't fail." Matt looked up at Sawyer. As they walked, they approached the far end of the pasture, and a couple of curious cows wandered toward them. "They think we have food," Matt told him, watching Sawyer reach out to touch their soft velvety noses, grateful for the change in topics. "It's all about food with them. And watch where you step." They were close enough to the house that he spotted Sabrina coming out of the covered cow shed. "Want to use the bathroom while we're up here?"

"Kinda?" Sawyer answered, and they both laughed, walking toward the big house.

Sabrina joined them that afternoon, carrying fishing poles and sandwiches to their campsite. Matt laughed as Sawyer waded into the water, getting his jeans wet. "You're nuts," Sabrina told him, incredulous. "That water's freezing."

Sawyer scoffed. "It's not that bad." He cast his line again, laughing. "I think I had a nibble there." In the end they caught two trout, both too small to eat, so they tossed them back into the river. "You two spending another night out here, or are you coming back to civilization tonight?" She quirked an eyebrow as she set the fishing poles in the back of Sawyer's truck.

Matt looked at Sawyer. "What do you think?"

"I'm ready to go back inside. That sound alright?" Sawyer slung an arm around Matt's shoulder, looking at him for an answer.

Matt grinned, trying not to lean into Sawyer's firm body and ignoring the smirk on Sabrina's face. "Yeah, I'm ready. Let's go get our stuff."

· · · · ● ● · · · ·

Friday night at the ranch wasn't any more exciting than normal, but having Sawyer around added something special. "I can't remember the last time I worked on a puzzle." Sawyer fixated on his section, a garden of wildflowers. "Do you see any more yellow pieces?"

"Grandma's always got one going here. It's tradition." Matt concentrated on his pond, but he slid over all the pieces with yellow on them he found.

"It's the only time anyone ever uses the dining room table," Sabrina added as she joined them, carrying a pitcher of a bright orange concoction and cups. "I made margaritas. Taste this and tell me what you think." She poured some into cups and handed one to each of them.

Matt took a sip. "It's sweet, but it's good. Fill me up."

She smiled, then looked over at Sawyer. "Chef's opinion matters here."

He chuckled. "Mango, right? I like it."

"Yep," she said proudly. "I like it too." Setting the pitcher down on the table, she started helping with the puzzle. "So, what do you think of the ranch?" she asked Sawyer.

"It's incredible. Matt says you and your grandfather do it all. I'm so impressed."

Sabrina's face went pink at the compliment. "It isn't easy work, but I can't imagine doing anything else. I only wish," she began, then stopped. "Well, it isn't quite what it used to be. I'd like to build up the business part of it again."

"Cows?" Matt recalled their conversation earlier in the week.

She shook her head. "I don't really care for all the work that comes with cattle. But I've been looking into other ways to bring in money."

"Eggs," Sawyer said as he fit two pieces of his puzzle together.

Matt and Sabrina looked at each other. "Eggs?" she repeated.

"Free-range chicken eggs. All the rage at the farmer's markets." Looking up at them, Sawyer grinned. "I bet you could also find a farmer's co-op or CSA that would buy them from you, or you could get customers to drive out here and pick them up."

Sabrina's eyes lit up with curiosity. "Tell me more."

••••••••••

Matt woke up later than usual on Saturday morning, the sun streaming through his window. Looking outside, he spotted all three dogs running back from the barn, Biscuit's little legs running double time just to keep up. As usual, Sabrina was already up and working, walking from the barn out to the pasture. When he opened his bedroom door, he inhaled deeply. The delicious breakfast smells only reinforced the fact that everyone else was up and moving. After using the bathroom, he walked to the kitchen, where Elena and Sawyer were standing over the stove, talking. "Morning." He rubbed his eyes as he wandered over.

"*Buenos dias, mijo*," Elena said. "Coffee's made."

Matt made it to the coffee machine and reached for his mug. "What are you making?"

"Migas," Sawyer said, snapping another picture with his camera. "Your grandma's showing me how she makes them."

Elena grinned, and Matt noticed she'd styled her hair and was wearing lipstick. "Sawyer's going to blog my pictures. Get some authentic recipes out there on the internet." She added the tomatoes and corn tortillas to the scrambled eggs and began stirring it all together. "This is even better when you make your own tortillas," she told them both. "Mateo, you should learn this too. What are you going to do when I'm not around to make this for you?"

"Well, that's never happening." Matt leaned in and kissed her cheek before sitting back down on a bar stool at the island, sipping his coffee. "What's happening outside?" He heard Sabrina's voice calling out to their grandfather, and his voice answering back. "Are they cleaning out the barn?"

"They got a bee in their bonnet about chickens. I think they're measuring space for chicken coops." She made a face, side-eying Sawyer, who bit his lip. "I know it's a good business plan, but I don't like chickens. We had them when I was little, and I just never..." She shook her head, murmuring something in Spanish.

Sawyer asked more questions about how Elena made her tortillas, and she described her recipe, preparing the *masa harina* and using her trusty ancient tortilla press.

"Next time you come, *mijo*, I'll show you," she said, wrapping an arm around him in a tight hug.

Sawyer's slow smile lit up his face, and Matt couldn't look away.

December

To: All_Staff_HaysMS
From: Curtis White
Date: December 8
Subject: Faculty Christmas party

The Hays Middle School Hospitality Committee is hosting the annual Christmas party this year on Friday, December 22nd at 7 pm at Grill Masters on Eleventh St. The cost is $15 per person for an all-you-can-eat barbecue buffet. Tea and soft drinks are included. Please RSVP to April Ford by Wednesday, December 20th, so we can have an accurate headcount.

– – –

Curtis White
Principal, Sarah Hays Middle School

· · · ● · ● · · · ·

Matt: *Are you awake? Sorry I'm texting so late. I don't know what hit me, but I'm sick. Not going in tomorrow. Any chance you're available?*

Sawyer: *Got a last-minute cancellation. I'm free tomorrow and Thursday if you need both days to get better.*

Matt: *Thanks S, I owe you one. They're taking a test*

in all the classes. It's already printed and ready to go.
Seating charts in a binder on my desk.

Sawyer: *Mr. Ahead of the Game. I'll take care of*
things. You just get better.

·· • • • • • • • ··

Matt first suspected it'd been the takeout he'd picked up Tuesday night that made him sick. Maybe the fish was bad, fried in old oil or something. Whatever it was, it took him down hard and fast, vomiting late into the night until there was nothing left to come up, with chills and fever thrown in for good measure. Later, he discovered from Cora that Clint and the basketball players also had it and he felt a little better, deciding it was one of those stomach bugs that got passed around, especially during the winter months at schools, and not food poisoning. Whatever it was, Matt couldn't recall being this sick in a long time and he spent two wretched days on his sofa under his favorite quilt, trying not to move.

By Friday, Matt still wasn't a hundred percent stronger, but he didn't want to be gone from his classes for three days in a row, particularly not at the start of a brand-new unit and not when he had five classes' worth of tests to grade. When Matt realized he'd be out two days, he'd asked Sylvia, who taught the other sections of eighth grade math, to come up with an independent assignment appropriate for his eighth graders and algebra students to work on Thursday, since all of them had tested on Wednesday. But when he got back to his classroom, he discovered Sawyer had not only graded the tests, but he'd also separated his classes into two groups: those who'd done well on their tests and worked on the independent activity, and those who could use a little revision and needed more time to finish their tests. It's what Matt would've done had he been there, and it inched up his respect for Sawyer that much more, as did his neat notes on how each class went, who was absent, who was acting up, and anything else he needed to know.

There was also a note left on top of his substitute binder: *Left a present for you in the fridge, green containers ~S.*

"Welcome back."

Matt gave a tired wave as he entered the teacher's lounge. "Thanks," he said, shuffling inside and finding his usual chair. He opened his insulated bag, then remembered the note. Standing, Matt walked to the fridge and, sure enough, there was a plastic bag with two green containers pushed to the back. Opening one, he grinned. "Chicken soup." Even though Matt hadn't been able to keep much down the last couple of days, maybe today he'd be able to enjoy lunch. He warmed one container and made his way back to his chair, settling in slowly and taking a careful spoonful, sighing to himself, content and oblivious to the glances of his coworkers.

"Taste good?" Alicia asked, grinning as she tucked into her salad.

"It does, thanks for asking." Matt inhaled it faster than was probably safe, but suddenly he was hungry, and it tasted amazing. "Anything interesting happen while I was out?" Matt finished his soup and listened to the usual lunchroom gossip from the past couple of days—who'd gotten in trouble, whose parents were on the warpath, which teacher had "forgotten" their afternoon duty for the third straight week.

"Sawyer said your kids did good for him. You've got them trained up right." Steve grinned. "He's a good sub."

"That he is," Matt agreed. "Definitely a good guy."

Kristine looked up. "Do you know if he's seeing anyone?"

The table got quiet, and Matt realized this was a circuitous way of asking if they were fucking. "Not that I know of," Matt answered with an offhand casualness he was sure fooled no one. And he was right. "Why are you asking?"

She shrugged. "My brother's coming into town for the holidays, and he just got over a nasty breakup. Thought maaaaybe I could give him Sawyer's number and they could get together, and you know. Hang out."

Alicia grinned. "You're awful." Soon the conversation moved back to another teacher who'd just ended a relationship and was over-sharing embarrassing details on her social media. Matt tuned out, shifting images of Sawyer going on a date with someone else out of his head. It wasn't his business who Sawyer spent his time with.

Nope.

· · • • • • • · · ·

Matt: *Thanks for the soup. Literally saved my life.*

Sawyer: *Don't mention it. Hey I had an idea. Robotic Club. How come you haven't started one yet? We had one at my high school.*

Matt: *Never thought about it. That's a really great idea.*

Sawyer: *I have them occasionally. Glad you're feeling better.*

· · • • • • • · · ·

The annual Hays faculty Christmas party was a highlight of the year. The Hospitality Committee always put on an excellent luncheon spread for the staff on the last day before the holiday break, but the party that evening was entertaining enough that most of the staff attended year after year. They rotated restaurants and this year they'd chosen Grill Masters, a local barbecue joint. Matt walked in with his Secret Santa gift, a bottle of rum he'd purchased for Felipe, whose name he'd drawn. Crystal Moss, one of the girl's coaches, had drawn his name and delivered his gift, a pair of slippers and a gift card, earlier that day at school, since she couldn't attend the party that night.

The hostess led him through the main dining area and into the private room in the back, where their party was being held. Matt grinned, seeing his coworkers dressed in holiday apparel and lined up at the buffet tables, others already seated and eating.

They still grouped by department, out of habit and familiarity. Matt spotted his math team camped out at a couple of long tables in the back. Matt waved at the coaching staff as he passed by and promised to stop by later before he headed to meet his coworkers and their families.

After shaking hands with Deanna's husband, Braydon, Matt settled into a chair across from Sylvia, Alex, and his wife, Joyce, already digging into their plates. "How's the food?"

"Eh," Alex answered. "It's okay."

Sylvia rolled her eyes. "But there's lots of it."

"Oh yeah, it's a nice buffet. Go get your food; we'll hold these seats for you."

Matt went over to the buffet and filled his plate with brisket, sausage, and potato salad before stepping back to the table. "It's a good-sized crowd this year." He tasted the food from his plate and had to agree with Alex; not the best barbecue in town, but a good price for an all-you-could-eat buffet. Soon, the entire table was laughing and telling anecdotes about their last few days, and plans they had for the forthcoming two weeks.

"How did you do on your final exams?" Deanna asked him.

Matt grinned. "One was a test and one was a paper. Got As in both classes, grades posted today." The table cheered, soft drinks raised in honor of Matt's accomplishment. Just then, he heard his name being shouted from the other side of the room. Turning his head, he saw Cora walking toward him.

"Matt!" She rested her hand on his shoulder. "Merry Christmas!"

"You too, Cora. How're you doing?"

"We're good! Look who I brought with me."

Matt turned and saw Sawyer behind her, wearing a silly Christmas sweater and jeans, talking to other teachers and being introduced to their significant others.

"Sawyer, where do you want to sit?" she asked.

"We've got room over here." Sylvia shifted over and made space for the late arrivals. "Go get your food first." Soon they sat down, plates heaping with food, and Matt found himself across from Sawyer. "How are you doing?" Sylvia passed down napkins to Sawyer and Cora. "Staying busy?"

Sawyer nodded. "I'm doing well. Phone's been ringing off the hook. I guess even teachers like to get started on their vacations a little early. And I went to the coast last weekend too, got a great video of the fishing boats bringing in shrimp."

Cora looked around. "Where's Dorothy?"

Deanna shook her head. "I don't think they wanted to take the baby out tonight. Too many people."

The table fell into small conversations, and Matt looked up and caught Sawyer watching him. "I'm glad you made it," Matt told him.

Sawyer laughed. "Cora said my presence was required. Also, I heard that last year, Alex got drunk and started singing dirty Christmas carols. Couldn't risk missing out on that."

Matt lifted his soft drink. "You'd regret it always."

After dinner, Matt walked around the other tables and visited friends. Steve and his wife ate with Alicia and Kristine, so he sat down for a few minutes before moving to the coach's table. He sat down with Paul and his wife, Clint and his girlfriend, and Bridget and her husband.

Paul reached over and tipped a healthy pour of amber liquid from a flask into Matt's soda. "Merry Christmas, Mateo."

"*Gracias, amigo*," Matt answered, taking a sip and recognizing the taste of Crown Royal. "Oh, this is the good stuff. Thanks." He took another sip.

"Hey, so we're going to Silverado's after this to have another couple of drinks. You're invited to join us."

Silverado's was your typical Texas honky-tonk bar and not Matt's kind of place, and he worried about being a third (or fifth) wheel, seeing the guys with their significant others. But the warm invitation touched him. "Yeah, that sounds good. I'll let you know." Soon they were chatting about Clint's latest fishing trip, but Matt kept looking back over at the math table, watching Sawyer. Watching how he talked with his hands. Watching the way his loose blond hair brushed his shoulders. Watching him smile at the conversations, and it might've been his imagination (or it might've been the whiskey) but Matt swore that every once in a while, Sawyer looked over at him and their eyes met, and Matt felt his face get hot.

That might also have been the whiskey.

Why not? the voice in his head murmured. *Just do it.*

Just do it.

Yes. Tonight, he'd do it. Why the fuck not?

After spending time with the coaches, Matt made it back to his table in time to see Sawyer standing and saying his goodbyes. "You're leaving?"

Sawyer nodded. "I think so. This has been fun, but I oughta go. I've got to be up early in the morning."

Matt raised an eyebrow but didn't ask. "Hey, can we talk for a moment? Somewhere quiet?"

"Yeah." Sawyer smiled. "As a matter of fact, I've got something for you, but it's in my truck."

Matt grinned, following him through the restaurant to the front parking lot. They walked outside, the air crisp and cold. "You didn't have to get me anything," Matt told him, approaching Sawyer's truck.

"Nah, man, I did. It's not much, just a little token of my gratitude, to thank you for helping me so much this fall. You've been a great friend, inviting me to hang out with your family." He handed Matt a gift bag.

Matt's heart started beating faster. "You didn't have to."

Sawyer nodded, his cheeks getting pink from the cold. "Yeah, I did."

Matt looked inside the bag, a short bark of laughter escaping him. "A cupcake pan?" He spotted a couple other baking utensils in there, along with candy sprinkles and cupcake paper liners. He laughed. "Oh, now I can make my own."

"It was the least I could do."

Matt shook his head. "But I was an ass."

"A little," Sawyer agreed, grinning. "But you had every reason. I showed up at a bad time."

"No, you were great." Matt held up his gift bag, holding it close to his chest. "You walked into our school and made a real difference. I mean, look," he said, pointing at the restaurant. "You're here at our Christmas party, unofficial staff. Practically family. And you did a lot for me too." Matt shifted from one leg to the other, swallowing. "Um, I don't have any sort of present for you here right now, but maybe we could go have dinner tomorrow night and I can make it up to you." He reached for Sawyer's hand, taking it in his and holding it. His heart beat loud in his chest, and Matt watched as Sawyer's eyes widened. "Just you and me."

Sawyer stared back at him, then he smiled but...it didn't quite reach his eyes. "Um," he began, biting his lip and tilting his head as he looked back at Matt.

Matt's heart pounded louder, the blood rushing from his head when he realized what was happening. Fuck. "I mean, only if you want to."

"No, no, it's not that," Sawyer stammered, as if trying to choose his words with care. "I do, you know I do. I'd like to go out and have dinner with you. Maybe more." There was a sad note in his voice. "But...I don't think it's a good idea."

Matt pulled his hand back. "Okay," he said. "No, it's okay. I'm sorry. I get it."

"No, you don't. Let me explain." Sawyer stepped closer, reaching out and taking Matt's hand in his. "I like you, Matt. I mean, I *really* like you. Anyone else, I'd have asked them out a month ago, maybe two. You're smart, funny, kind. You love your family." His smile faltered. "I could fall hard for you. Maybe..." Sawyer bit his lip again. "But I know you've got your plans and I know how important they are to you...and I don't think I fit in them. I would worry every day that I'd end up embarrassing you somehow, that you'd find out that you and me, us being together, would mess up all of your plans, and you'd hate me for holding you back. That I might not be enough."

"I would never hate you." But how much of what Sawyer said was true? Could Matt make space in his life for someone without resenting the time they took away from his plans?

"I hope not," Sawyer told him. "Believe it or not, I've thought about this a lot, you and me. What it'd be like, and for what it's worth, I think we could've been great together."

"Wait, Sawyer." Matt took a step closer as all the air left his lungs. He felt like someone had punched him. "You think you'd embarrass me?"

"It's like I said. I just showed up at a bad time. You've got a lot going on right now, Matt, and I don't think there's any room left in there for me." Leaning in close, Sawyer kissed his cheek. "Merry Christmas, Mateo."

Matt stood speechless. Stepping back from Sawyer's truck, he held on to his gift and watched Sawyer drive away.

Embarrassed? Was that what Sawyer thought? Matt wasn't embarrassed about his life or his choices. He didn't go out of his way to point out that he was different from other people, that he was gay, but that didn't mean it embarrassed him. Sawyer didn't understand. Or maybe...

Maybe he didn't want to be with him. "Well, that hurt." Matt murmured to himself, looking down at the gift bag in his hands. He walked to his truck and set the gift in the passenger seat. But instead of walking back inside and saying goodbye to his friends, he slid into the driver's seat of his truck.

Returning to the party was forgotten. Drinking with the coaches was forgotten. Matt pulled out of the parking lot and drove in the opposite direction of Sawyer, driving toward his house.

It was a long time before he fell asleep that night.

• • • • • • • • • •

Matt didn't decorate his house much for Christmas, other than a garland wreath on his door that he bought each year from the high school band boosters, and grocery store poinsettias for the kitchen table. He spent most of his holiday break at the ranch, so it never seemed important to buy a Christmas tree at his house, just for him. But Elena still put up a big tree each year, so he went over to help her set it all up, watching as she pulled old ornaments out of a plastic container and hung them with care, telling him the same stories each year about where each one came from.

If Matt was quieter than normal, she didn't mention it, but when they finished decorating, she hugged him tight, a little longer than normal, and kissed his cheek. "I love you, *mijo*."

Later that evening, Matt found her in the dining room, working on one of her jigsaw puzzles. This one was in the beginning stages of construction, just the edges and corner pieces connected. "What's this supposed to be?" Matt picked up the lid to the puzzle box and saw a white sand beach, palm trees swaying over a turquoise ocean. "Looks like Hawaii," he said, sitting down next to her. "At least that's what it looks like on TV."

"I don't know, I thought it was pretty." Elena peered into the box with all the pieces. She began pulling out all the blue pieces, then handed the box to Matt. "Give me all the blue ones you can find. Set them here." She patted an empty spot on the table.

He smiled at how seriously she took this and then obeyed her directive. "How are you and Grandpa doing?"

"We're fine. Your grandpa's allergies have been bothering him, but we both went to the doctor last week and he said we're good." She looked up from her puzzle at him. "And you? Are you okay? Sabrina said you had the flu a few weeks ago."

"I think it was a stomach bug," he said, setting the blue pieces picture-side up on the table. "I think this is all of them." She carefully arranged them, not by the various shades of blue but by shape, using the pattern of the water as a guide. Matt watched her process, picking up a piece and trying out all the possible interlocking possibilities, setting them down one after another. "You're not even looking to see if they match."

She laughed. "It's not about the picture. It's about the fit. I can tell if they fit together, just by the feel." Smiling as she found a match, she set them down and picked up another puzzle piece and began the process again. "The picture will sometimes deceive you, all those minor details mixing you up. But the way it feels, the way they snap together. That will never let you down." Giving a little giggle, she set down another pair. "See?"

"I guess you've got it down, Grandma."

She glanced over at him. "What's going on with you? You sound tired."

"Nothing." Matt kept his eyes focused on the puzzle. "Just been a busy year."

"And your friend?" she asked. "I hoped we might see him for Christmas."

Matt shook his head. "I think he's leaving town soon."

Elena's face showed her disappointment. "That's a shame. He seemed like a good man."

"The best," Matt agreed. Elena gave him a pointed look but said nothing as they worked on the puzzle in silence.

Later that night, Matt walked toward the kitchen to get something to drink when he spotted Sabrina sitting on the floor of the living room, gift bags and wrapping paper around her as she watched an old holiday movie on the television. "You look like an elf," he told her, finding a stray bow on the floor and setting it on her head as he walked by.

She wrinkled her nose. "You look like a scrooge. Did you need a couple little envelopes for your gift cards, or are you just going to hand them out to all of us again like last year? Or better yet, skip the middleman and give everyone a couple of twenties?"

"Many people appreciate being able to pick out their own gifts." Matt walked into the kitchen and opened the refrigerator. "Want a drink?" he called out to her.

"Yeah, surprise me."

He grabbed two orange sodas and closed the fridge. He walked back into the living room and set it down on the table next to her, sitting down. "What did you get me?"

"A gift card." She winked at him, tickling his leg. Then a warm smile fell over her face. "So, do I need to get a little gift for Sawyer? I hope he'll be joining us for Christmas."

Matt shook his head, glancing over at the television. "No, he won't."

Her face fell. "Oh, no. Does he have other plans?"

Matt shrugged. "I don't know. How would I know what he's doing?"

Sabrina rolled her eyes, exasperated. "What do you mean? I thought you two were friends."

"Well, we're not that kind of friends."

She blinked. "Why not? He's a sweet guy. You could do a lot worse."

"Sorry to disappoint you, but it's not like that. We're just *friends*," he repeated. "We're not even that close."

Her brows knotted up in confusion. "But you could be. C'mon, he liked you, I could tell. You could be more."

"No, we couldn't," Matt answered, his voice tight.

"But how will you know if you don't—"

"Because I did," Matt snapped, turning to look at her. "I asked him out. He said no."

Sabrina's face fell, and the room silent. "Oh God, I'm so sorry. I thought..."

He shrugged, taking a sip from his drink. "Me too. I mean, I know he does like me. But he told me it wouldn't work out. He said I'm too..." Matt paused, shaking his head. "He thinks I'd end up embarrassed by being with him, that a relationship would interfere with all my plans."

"Wait." Sabrina turned her body toward him. "Tell me exactly what happened." Matt started looking out the window, so she shook his leg. "I want to hear about this." She shifted up to sit on the sofa next to him. "Matty. Talk to me."

Matt didn't want to talk about it, and yet, he found himself telling her all about Sawyer. He told her about the day they'd met, and his irritation about having to do all this extra work. How they'd get to work early so Matt could teach him the math Sawyer would teach that day, and how they made cupcakes together one night. He told her about their camping down by the river, how he'd shared his feelings about growing up in Estrella, all the shit that had gone down with their mom, and how he felt when he had to give up the engineering program. Finally, he told her about Sawyer's Christmas gift to him, and how he'd asked him out, and how Sawyer had told him no.

Sabrina listened to all of this, her face showing her disappointment. She frowned. "Oh, Matt. He wants to be with you."

"Not enough," Matt answered. "And let's be honest, he's right. I'm not ready for any sort of actual relationship."

"That's bullshit. You're an amazing man, and anyone would be lucky to have you in their lives. Sawyer knows that." She reached over, squeezing his leg. "I just don't think you know that."

···•·•••··

Christmas day came, the four of them spending it together much the same as they had for many years. His family laughed when Matt passed out his gift cards. Sabrina gave him a new game for his PlayStation, and his grandparents gave him clothes and a new lawnmower for his house. Hector wore his old Santa hat and pulled a small jeweler's box out of his pocket, handing it to his wife. "Our fiftieth Christmas together, *querida*," he said, and Matt saw her open it and pull out a thick gold chain.

"Hector." Elena touched it gently, then leaned over and kissed him before putting it around her neck. Her hand cupped his cheek. "*Te amo, mi corazon.*"

Sabrina glanced at Matt, and he guessed she was thinking the same thing as he was—how lucky these two people had been to find each other, to spend a lifetime loving each other.

And...how sad it was they hadn't found the same.

It was a quiet Christmas evening. Matt took out the trash after they ate and looked up at the sky. He'd considered going camping. It had been fun when he and Sawyer had gone out on Thanksgiving, and it hadn't been a particularly cold Christmas day. But the wind had picked up throughout the day, and now he changed his mind. Instead, Matt went for a walk early the next morning, out to the spot where they'd camped, and sat on a long, flat rock, watching the sun coming up over the trees.

The sound of water and snapping twigs caught his attention. Matt saw a buck crossing the river, not fifty feet away. A big guy, twelve points from what Matt could see as he lifted his phone and took a quick picture.

Sawyer would love this, and Matt began texting him when he remembered—they weren't together. They weren't even friends, he guessed, since he'd heard nothing from Sawyer since that night a week ago.

He closed his phone. He could text it to Sabrina. His grandfather would like it. Cora might think it was interesting. Hell, Clint would be green with envy if he knew Matt had gotten that close.

Matt had friends, lots of friends. He wasn't lonely. Was he alone? Yeah, maybe, but it was still a good life. He had a job and his family and plans for the future and...

Matt snorted. His plans, that's what Sawyer had said. No time for anyone else because of "his plans." Was he right? Was Matt destined to end up successful and yet alone in the end? Sawyer hadn't been wrong when he'd asked why Matt didn't have his picket fence yet. There was a part of him that wanted that, someone to love, maybe a couple of kids. Someday.

But increasingly, every time he looked at his grandparents, it reminded him not only of their amazing love, but the glaring realization that he didn't have that and, at this rate, he never would. If he found someone tomorrow, the chances of spending fifty years with them were slim.

Why was he doing all of this if there wasn't anyone to share it with?

Every day for a week, Matt had this conversation with himself. Every night, he went to bed wondering how Sawyer was doing. What Sawyer was doing. If Sawyer might be someone special.

How would Matt ever know if he didn't try?

·· • • • • • • • ··

Sabrina had plans in town for New Year's Eve with friends. "Come with me." She wrapped a scarf around her neck as she got ready to leave. "It's going to be super chill, just board games and tequila shots."

He appreciated the offer, but after a week of asking himself those deep questions, he'd decided this was the night.

If you couldn't offer your heart to someone on New Year's Eve, then when?

·· • • • • • • • ··

Matt: *Can we talk?*

Matt held onto his phone, waiting for a response, hoping Sawyer didn't already have plans for the night.

He didn't have to wait long.

Sawyer: *Yeah. I'm home.*
Matt: *On my way. Be there in an hour.*

From the highway, Matt saw Sawyer's blue truck parked next to his RV. Taking a deep breath, he pulled into the trailer park and drove toward Sawyer's RV. He smiled, seeing strands of multicolored Christmas lights hanging from several of the RVs, including Sawyer's. Suddenly Matt was mad at himself for wasting these past weeks, not being in Sawyer's life.

He parked next to Sawyer's truck. It was clear and cold, so he zipped up his jacket as he stepped out of the truck. The light was on inside the trailer, but no one answered when he knocked.

Shit. Matt turned around, looking to see if maybe Sawyer was outside when he saw him walking back toward the Airstream, a bright yellow knit hat on his head, holding a leash and walking Biscuit, wearing a matching yellow harness. "Hey."

"Hey." Matt's heart pounded in his chest. "Sorry to bother you so late."

"No, it's good. I just— They needed help getting started." Sawyer pointed at a group of people standing around a barbecue grill. Turning back to Matt, he grinned. "Happy New Year."

"You too." Matt heard fireworks going off outside of the RV park, kids running by with sparklers in their hands. "Can we talk?"

"Yeah." Sawyer opened the door and let Biscuit back inside the trailer. "Um, you want to talk inside? Is it too cold out here?"

"I'm okay." Matt nodded, rubbing his hands together. "It's just..." All his words, his prepared speech, began slipping through his fingers. "Sometimes I come off as an ass, I know that. I'm not the most charming guy, and I let my goals run my life when I should let people in. Letting you in."

Sawyer frowned. "You shouldn't change who you are for anyone."

"But...that's not true." Matt breathed in, his lungs filling with the cold air. "I absolutely should change when I'm wrong, and according to everyone I know, I'm wrong. I'm ruining my life not being with you. Not touching you and kissing you and waking up next to you. None of these plans are worth it if I let you walk away from me like that again. We gotta give it a chance," Matt said. "What if...what if this is it?"

Sawyer stared at him, bright blue eyes wide as more fireworks began shooting off, the park lighting up with bright colorful displays. "This can't be about what your friends want, or what your family wants. What is it that you want, Matt?" His breath condensed in the cold.

He was fucking this up. "Sawyer." Matt licked his lips. "Nothing's felt right since you said what you said."

"Matt—"

"No, not like that. You were right. I've got this plan in my head, but there's a big hole in the middle, and that's where you belong. I can change, Sawyer. You're worth making the change." Sawyer didn't look any happier. "It's a new year, a perfect time to start over. Please let me start all this over with you. That's what I want." He reached one hand up and rested on Sawyer's chest. "Nothing means more to me right now than making you happy. Please give me that chance."

Sawyer's mouth turned up, a slow smile that made it to his eyes. "Are you sure this is worth it?"

Matt reached for Sawyer's hands, tugging him closer. "I've never been surer of anything."

Sawyer's smile widened. "Didn't peg you for the corny type, Ruiz," he said, tilting his head closer to Matt's face.

"I'm full of surprises." In all the time they'd known each other, they'd never been this close. Matt saw little freckles on Sawyer's cheeks, flecks of gold in his blue eyes, framed by dark golden lashes. A man's face, not beautiful or porcelain, but a man with his hard edges and stubbled skin. His hand cupped Sawyer's rough cheek. "Happy New Year."

Sawyer smiled at him, wrapping his arms around Matt. "Happy New Year."

Matt tilted his head up and they kissed, the barest brush of their lips that set his nerves on fire. They kissed again, soft and tender. "Can we go inside?"

"Yeah." Sawyer took Matt's hands and guided him into the RV. The door closed behind them, and then Sawyer's arms wrapped around him, and he closed his eyes as Sawyer kissed his neck.

Matt groaned. Sawyer pulled back, kissing Matt's forehead. Matt noticed a few changes to the RV since the last time he'd been here. He saw a small Christmas tree and decorations, and a new rug in the kitchen area. Biscuit was curled up in a ball on the sofa. She opened her eyes when they entered the trailer, wagging her tail when she saw them, and then went back to sleep.

Sawyer took off his jacket and tossed it on the sofa. "Sorry, it's kinda cold in here. I've got a heater over there," he said, pointing at his bed.

Now it was Matt's turn to grin. "That's a hell of a pickup line. 'Hey, are you cold? It's warm over by my bed.'" He stood close to Sawyer. "Does it usually work?"

"I'll let you know in the morning." Sawyer pulled Matt close and then they kissed again, deeper and hungrier. "Tell me what you want."

Matt wanted a lot. He slid his hands under Sawyer's hoodie, touching warm, smooth skin. "This," he murmured as Sawyer's mouth found his neck again, a hot tongue tracing along his pulse point. He pulled off Sawyer's hair tie, threading his fingers through those long, soft strands. "I want you so fucking bad."

"Okay." Sawyer pulled back and rested his forehead against Matt. Taking him by the hand, he led Matt over toward his bed and sat down, spreading his legs so Matt could stand between them. Matt didn't often look down at Sawyer, and from this perspective he appeared younger, even more boyish. "What are you thinking?" Sawyer asked, his hands settling on Matt's hips.

"Fuck, so many things. But right now..." Matt tugged Sawyer's hoodie over his head. "I mostly want to see your ink up close and personal." They both laughed, kissing again. Matt traced over the tattoos on Sawyer's shoulders, intricate patterns mixed with chef's knives and assorted vegetables.

Sawyer's eyes closed as Matt touched his arms and chest. "Anything I need to know before we..." He opened his eyes, looking up at Matt. "Before anything happens?"

"Yeah." Matt sat down next to him and brushed their lips together. "Sometimes I get a little ticklish." They laughed again, levity mixed in with their sexual energy, and all of Matt's nerves melted away. Soon their clothes lay tossed into a pile on the floor. Sawyer's hands were everywhere, touching and gripping and holding Matt's body like he owned it, endless kisses as they learned each other's bodies. It was perfect.

Except... "Hey, babe." Matt lifted Sawyer's chin, their eyes meeting. He nodded over at the sofa, the dog staring at them. "Is she going to watch the entire time?"

"I fucking hope not." Sawyer's blue eyes were bright with mirth as he rolled them over. He dropped soft kisses along Matt's body and slid down between his legs.

Afterward, Matt lay on his side, looking out a small window next to Sawyer's bed. Long arms wrapped around him, and Matt felt Sawyer kiss the back of his neck as they lay under a thick blanket.

Sawyer reached his hand around and laced their fingers together. "You okay?"

"I'm good. I'm great." Matt smiled, pressing back against that firm body. Turning around, he wrapped his arms around Sawyer, pressing baby kisses on his cheeks, his nose, his mouth. This felt even more intimate than what they'd just done, and

Matt couldn't remember the last time he'd lingered like this with a lover, with no intention of moving. "How 'bout you?"

Sawyer groaned, their legs tangling. "Amazing." One more kiss, and he rested his head against Matt's shoulder. "You're amazing. That was even better than I imagined."

"You imagine much?" Matt's fingers threaded through Sawyer's hair.

"You've got no idea." Matt looked into Sawyer's eyes, seeing all those emotions he felt reflected back at him. Sawyer leaned in and kissed Matt's nose. "You need to leave?"

Matt shook his head. "Pretty sure you're going to make me breakfast in the morning." They kissed again. "I'm not missing out on that."

January

D ata exists that show restorative discipline can work effectively when used with fidelity, but what are teacher attitudes toward these practices that place much of the burden back on their shoulders? Most responses have been positive. However, teachers expressed the need for more initial and—

Matt hung his head. The word was on the tip of his tongue, right out of reach. Maybe that meant it was time for a rest. Rolling his shoulders, he pushed back away from his desk and stretched, arms raised upward. When he shifted to take a step, he had to tiptoe over Biscuit, snoring next to him. "Don't let me interrupt you," he murmured to the Yorkie, who cracked open one eye and yawned before closing it again. Lovely. A quiet rain tapped on the side of the house. A gray and gloomy weekend, and Matt guessed maybe the dog had the right idea.

He reached for his coffee mug and wandered into the kitchen. He couldn't help that indescribable emotion he had, seeing Sawyer sitting on his sofa, folding towels while watching something on the television. It felt like playing house, spending the weekend together, the two of them and the dog. They'd spent all day Saturday clearing out Matt's garage and putting up new shelving, then had fallen asleep in a tangle after Matt had received the best blow job in the shower he'd ever experienced. The next morning, Sawyer had made them a hearty Sunday morning breakfast and then had started doing his laundry with Matt's washing machine while Matt had gotten to work on his research paper.

He walked over and refilled his coffee mug. "Need some help?"

"Did you finish?" Sawyer made a tidy pile of towels inside his basket.

"Almost?" Matt sat on the arm of the sofa and leaned in for a kiss. "Just taking a break."

Sawyer leaned back, away from his face. "You get a kiss when you're finished."

Matt sighed. "That's mean."

"Tough love." Sawyer reached over and gave him a peck on the cheek. "I'll have a surprise for you for late lunch, but you gotta go finish."

"I will. I needed to stretch my legs." Biscuit trotted down the hallway, peering around as if she'd woken up and realized she was alone. "Look who's awake."

"What's your paper about?" Sawyer petted the sofa next to him, watching as Biscuit jumped up and started gazing at Matt. "Traitor," he said affectionately, stroking her back.

"She's a good girl." Matt reached out and petted the dog as well. He settled on the other side of the sofa, smirking as Biscuit scrambling toward him, jumping into his lap. "The paper is about campus discipline."

"That's important in a school. Do you think you'll enjoy doing that kind of work more than teaching the kids, when you give up teaching?"

Matt shrugged. "It's part of the job of an administrator. Running the school, dealing with broader issues. It's important work."

"Didn't say it wasn't," Sawyer answered. "I asked if that was how you wanted to spend your days. You're great with the kids. You explain these concepts in ways that make it easier to understand."

"Thanks." Matt felt warm at the compliment. "It's fun watching them understand and then applying it. Sometimes I hear about former students, the ones in high school already and how they're succeeding. It feels good knowing I was a part of that." His first group of kids was starting college. That was something to think about. "But I never wanted to teach forever. There was always a higher goal."

"Running a school district," Sawyer said, reaching for a pile of socks.

"Making a difference. Maybe I can help teach the teachers how to be successful. It would affect kids too," he added.

"Agreed. Just..." Sawyer rested one hand on Matt's arm. "I think..." He paused, then continued. "Work should be more than an achievement. It should satisfy you as well, the day-to-day parts of the job. You should want to get up each day and keep going."

"There's nothing wrong with having goals."

"I don't disagree with that." Sawyer leaned in and kissed Matt, soft and sweet. "The key is making sure you've got the right goals."

By later than afternoon, Matt had written a good chunk of the paper. Satisfied, he emerged from his office and spotted Sawyer and his dog stretched out long on the living room sofa. They were both sleeping while a British cooking show played quietly in the background. The light rain hadn't let up, and the house was cool, the scent of something warm wafting from the kitchen. Matt picked up an old quilt from the loveseat and covered Sawyer, and then settled down with his phone. He took a quick picture of them before opening one of his mobile game apps and started playing. Twenty minutes went by, and the oven timer began chiming.

Sawyer blinked his eyes open. "Is that the timer?"

"Yeah," Matt said. "And it smells incredible." Biscuit had migrated to his lap, and he carefully shifted her off him so he could follow Sawyer into the kitchen to check out whatever was cooking. "This is just for the two of us, right?" he asked as Sawyer removed a massive pan of lasagna out of the oven. "You don't have a family somewhere I don't know about?"

Sawyer laughed. "I wanted enough so we'd have lunches this week. I'm working three days at the high school, and you can have a brief vacation from your ham sandwiches."

"They will be missed, it must be said." Matt reached into the cabinet and found two plates. "But somehow I'll manage." He began setting the table while Sawyer quickly put a pan of garlic bread in the oven to heat and pulled a green salad out of the fridge. Soon they were sitting down and eating, Matt's expression of one of satisfaction and a little amazement. "You just threw this together?" Matt stared in amazement and asked himself why he didn't cook like this more often.

"It's not that hard, making lasagna, if you have the right ingredients." Sawyer's face lit up when he saw Matt eating, reminding him of a similar expression on his grandma's face sometimes. Satisfaction...or maybe something more intimate.

"Well, it's amazing. You're really talented," Matt told him. "This makes you happy, feeding people?"

Sawyer looked over at him, chewing slowly. "I never thought about it like that. I know it feels good, seeing all these separate ingredients come together into this." Sawyer pointed at the lasagna in the pan. "It's like alchemy, in a way. That's cool, and I enjoy seeing that happen." Reaching over, he wiped a bit of sauce off Matt's jaw. "It feels great when people say it tastes good too."

"My alchemist." Matt smiled, leaning close and kissing him. Thunder rumbled outside, both men turning toward the window. "Gonna start storming soon."

Sawyer frowned. "That's my cue to take off. I don't want to get caught outside in a downpour with all my clean clothes and the dog."

It was on the tip of Matt's tongue to ask Sawyer to stay another night, to tell him he could get up extra early in the morning and drive home to change, or just leave from Matt's house. But spending the night was one thing; were they ready for two nights in a row? How soon before that became a week or longer? "You get your lasagna for lunches. I've got extra plastic containers. We can put some of this salad in a plastic bag too."

Soon Sawyer bundled himself up, little Biscuit leashed and tucked under Sawyer's jacket, while Matt carried the laundry baskets over to Sawyer's truck, setting them on the passenger side as Sawyer climbed behind the wheel.

"Good thing you're not on the bicycle."

"Can you imagine?" Sawyer grinned, pushing Biscuit off his lap, and leaned over to kiss Matt goodbye. Matt glanced around and didn't notice anyone, but Sawyer seemed to catch on to Matt's discomfort. "I'll call you later. Thanks, babe." Sawyer rolled the window up and pulled out of the driveway, and Matt walked back into a house that now felt too big for just him.

••••••••••

"All I know is she was sitting in the middle of the living room next to this dead bird, staring up at me like I should be thankful she's contributing to the household." Kristine laughed as she presented her phone, revealing a photograph of her cat and a floor covered in feathers. "Can you believe this?"

"Knowing your luck, yeah, I do. Now, what I want to know is," Cynthia asked, pointing at Matt's lunch, "does that lasagna taste as amazing as it smells? Because it smells amazing."

Matt looked up from his plastic container, noting that they were all glancing at him. He couldn't mask the smile on his face as he ate. "It does. Heats pretty good too."

"Spoiled rotten, that's what you are, having a boyfriend who's a brilliant chef." But the affection in Cynthia's voice told Matt his colleagues were happy for him while not being intrusive.

Well, not too intrusive. "Do you know if Sawyer's available to sub this Friday?" Alicia asked. "I think we're going to go visit my parents."

Matt shook his head. "I don't know. Send him a text and see what he's up to."

"I'll text him later." She smiled, soft and knowing. "I'm glad he's still here."

Matt chuckled lightly, taking another bite. "Me too."

"Do you think he's sticking around for a while?" Steve asked.

"I don't know." Matt paused for a moment. It was a question he'd asked himself a few times since they'd started dating. "We haven't— I mean, we've only been going out a couple of weeks." It felt like longer, Matt knew, but this relationship was still brand new, and sometimes he still didn't believe they were together.

"Well, I hope he sticks around," Alicia said, "and not just because he's a great substitute."

· · · · ● ● ● ● · · ·

Matt swung by his favorite burger place and picked up dinner for the two of them. Pulling a hot fry out of the bag, he blew on it before taking a bite, still somehow burning his tongue. A little after six in the evening, Matt drove toward Sawyer's place, the winter sun going down early. Although Sawyer came to his house regularly, Matt had made this trip a few times now. He parked next to Sawyer's truck and stepped out, chuckling at Sawyer's neighbors. Late January, and Miss Amanda still had her Christmas lights on her trailer, twinkling colorful and bright as he parked his truck. Festive.

He grabbed the food and drinks, closing the door to his truck with his foot and walking toward the trailer. He heard Biscuit scrambling around inside as he stepped up toward the door, knocking twice. "Hey, babe," he called out, laughing when the door opened and he saw Sawyer's bright smile. "I made dinner."

Sawyer looked down at the fast-food bags. "You made burgers?" He grinned, kissing Matt's cheek as he stepped inside and got comfortable.

Matt took the food out of the bags, separating them into two piles. "The cheeseburger is for you. The other one is mine." Matt picked up his meal and sat down at the small kitchen table. Looking around, he spotted the sink full of dirty dishes and Sawyer's video camera positioned in filming mode. "So, what were you up to this afternoon?" he asked, taking a bite of his burger. "Looks like a tornado rolled through here."

Sawyer rolled his eyes and sat down next to him, eating his fries two at a time. "Flan," he said proudly. "It took a couple of tries to get it looking good, but the custard tasted amazing. Right now it's cooling in the fridge. Sorry I had to ask you to bring me dinner, but I didn't think it'd take as long as it did. If you can stay, you can be my guinea pig later." Taking another fry, Sawyer held it out in front of Matt's mouth. "I'll reward you handsomely for your efforts, and for dinner."

"You got a deal." They ate quickly, both of them hungry from their respective long days. "Tell me about how you—" he began, interrupted by the sound of his phone ringing. A quick glance informed him it was his grandmother. "Hey, give me a minute really quick, okay?" Matt stood and held up his phone. "It's Grandma."

"Oh yeah, go for it," Sawyer said. "I can step outside if you need privacy, or..."

Matt shook his head. What was he going to say that this man couldn't hear? "Don't worry about it. I'll sit over there in the living room." He stepped past Sawyer, who swatted his ass as he passed, and settled on the sofa three feet away.

Lifting the phone to his face, he angled his body away from Sawyer so he wouldn't laugh. "Hey, Grandma, what's up?" Matt stretched out, reaching over to pet the small dog who'd ambled over toward him as he listened to her talk about her day. "Wait, what did you say?"

"I asked if you remembered Mr. Ramon. He passed away a few days ago, and we're going to go to Floresville for the funeral on Friday."

"Oh, I'm sorry to hear that. I remember him. He was a nice man."

"He was. But I wanted to ask you about Saturday as well."

Matt's eyes widened as she told him about her proposed weekend plans. "Um, let me ask him. I bet he'll like that." He saw Sawyer clearing their fast-food trash. "Well, tell Grandpa I said hey, and I'll see you guys soon."

He put the phone down and glanced at Sawyer, watching as he dried the clean dishes with a small towel and placed everything in its spot in his well-organized kitchen. He stepped behind Sawyer and wrapped his arms around him. "You busy next weekend?"

Sawyer's brows furrowed, and he chewed on his bottom lip. "Well, off the top of my head, I don't seem to have anything urgently pressing." Turning his body, he looked down at Matt and asked, "Everything okay?"

"Yeah. Well, not all good news. A friend of the family passed away."

"Oh shit," Sawyer murmured. "Someone you knew?"

"Yeah, I remember him from when I was a kid." Matt remembered a kind man with a missing tooth who used to share Tootsie Rolls with him. "Someone who used to work with my grandpa at the ranch. Stroke, it sounds like."

"That's too bad," Sawyer said, kissing his forehead.

Matt agreed, sitting back down on the sofa. "Anyhow, I asked about next weekend because my grandma wants to make tamales. It's a ...mass assembly-like production." Matt laughed softly. "And she thought you might like to learn."

"Absolutely." Sawyer lit up. "That sounds like fun."

Matt arched a brow. "I'll ask you again about two hours into the entire process. Still," he admitted, "we'll have enough for a few months. It's always worth it in the end." He tipped his face up for a kiss when Sawyer leaned in. "You mentioned something about a reward earlier?"

Sawyer laughed. "Mind like a steel trap. Yeah, and it should be chilled enough by now." One more kiss, and Sawyer stepped back toward the kitchen and opened the fridge. Pulling out a tray, he carefully set it down on the counter, several small custard discs sitting in baking cups. "Honest opinion. Tell me what you think."

Matt stood and walked over, leaning against Sawyer, who plated one of the small flans. "Looks good," he said, reaching a finger down into the caramel liquid dripping on the small plate. "Gimme a fork."

Sawyer found two forks. "Sit." He walked back to the sofa and handed the fork and plate to Matt, watching Matt's face as he scooped a bit of the creamy custard into his mouth. "What do you think?"

"I think it's amazing." Matt closed his eyes at the taste, the custard melting on his tongue. Not too sweet, just a hint of salt in the caramel. The custard set perfectly. "This is good. You get videos?" he asked, taking another bite.

Sawyer nodded. "And pictures. Gonna use this for the next episode if it turned out okay."

"Better than okay, babe. Two thumbs up." Matt took another bite, licking custard off his lips.

Sawyer pumped his fist, satisfied with his results. "Score." They finished it quickly, Matt holding up his fork to Sawyer's mouth, feeding him the last bite. "Do you need to leave soon?" he asked, those muscular hands sliding up Matt's legs, resting on his hips.

Matt let out a soft groan. "Greedy. I've got a few minutes."

Sawyer tugged him onto his lap, facing him. "Might need more than a few minutes."

Matt's knees spread open on either side of him, straddling Sawyer, their faces close. He rubbed their noses together. "Is that a promise?" he asked, their lips brushing against each other. Sawyer groaned, and Matt felt those hands slip under his shirt.

"Now who's greedy?" They kissed, softly at first, but growing deeper until they were out of breath. "Stand up."

Matt slid off Sawyer's lap, his hands settling on the man's shoulders. Sawyer's hands unbuckled Matt's belt, then worked at the buttons on his pants. Matt could see Sawyer's chest rising and falling with each breath, his eyes widening as he pulled Matt's khakis down. Pressing his face forward, he nuzzled Matt's cock through his boxer briefs. "Fuck," Matt groaned, looking down at them, his cock hard and aching at the sight. He pulled at the hair tie holding Sawyer's hair back, spreading it around as Sawyer pulled his cock free and took the head into his mouth.

He held Sawyer's head in place, slowly fucking his mouth. Sawyer gripped his hips, one hand sliding down to grasp the base of Matt's cock. Matt felt that tension in his belly pooling, tightening his grip on Sawyer's hair. It wouldn't take long. "Almost there," he murmured; hips pumped faster, fucking that sinful mouth until he stilled, emptying himself down Sawyer's throat.

Unbelievable. Matt rolled his head back, catching his breath, but only long enough for Sawyer to yank his pants off completely. Sawyer stood and lifted Matt, wrapping Matt's legs around him and kissing him as he carried him back toward his bed.

"At least you've gotten over the dog watching us." Sawyer reached over the side of his bed and turned on his small space heater, then lay back down, pressing a kiss into Matt's hair. "I'm proud of you. That's growth."

Matt snorted, leaning into that powerful body. "I'm broadening my horizons." They kissed again, and Matt rolled over, the blanket pooling at his waist as he sat up. "I should go. Got a busy day tomorrow."

"Okay." Sawyer rubbed small circles on Matt's back. "You know…" There was a pause, long enough for Matt to wonder if Sawyer had forgotten what he was saying. After a moment, he went on. "Maybe this summer you could go on a trip with me. We could take the RV out for a spin, see the sights."

Matt surprised himself by not immediately panicking or speculating on what this all meant. "I've got a lot of things going on this summer," he said in a matter-of-fact tone, because he did. At least two graduate classes, maybe more, if the university offered the right ones. "But it sounds like fun." Sawyer's face had lost a little of that sparkle, so he leaned over and kissed him, tugging at his bottom lip with his teeth. "I bet we could do a quick trip somewhere." It wasn't the idea of the trip that he objected to, or the person he'd travel with. It was the time commitment Matt wasn't sure he could make.

Sawyer smiled at him, but with a lingering wariness, as if he didn't quite believe Matt. "Sounds like a plan." He took a deep breath and sat up next to Matt. "Thanks for coming over tonight." He kissed Matt's shoulder and handed him his shirt. "And thanks for dinner."

"The flan was great," Matt told him. "And so are you." They kissed again, gentle, Sawyer's hands threading through Matt's short hair. "Call me tomorrow?"

"Will do." Sawyer watched as he dressed, the softest expression on his face. "Drive home safe, babe." Then he laughed, reaching for Math's hand, bringing it to his lips and kissing his knuckles. "And for fuck's sake, please take some of that flan with you."

· · • • • • • • · ·

Matt couldn't remember the last time he'd made the trip out to the ranch as a passenger. "I don't think it's that big a deal."

"I know you don't. But it is to me." Sawyer looked into the rearview mirror, checking on Biscuit, who sat calmly in the backseat next to their traveling bags. "How much do your grandparents know about us?"

"Enough to invite you over to make tamales. Babe, I'm almost thirty years old. Having an overnight guest stay in my room will not be a shock to them."

"Still." Sawyer shook his head. "I'm not that comfortable with it. Let's just say that for right now, I'm staying in the guest room unless, I don't know, maybe your grandmother's got all kinds of sewing projects around that she doesn't want moved."

"Whatever you want." Matt smirked, but Sawyer's reaction touched him. For someone with a complicated relationship with his own family, Sawyer was quite fond of Matt's grandparents and sister. That he showed so much respect to them made Matt's heart melt. "But for the record, you're adorable."

Sawyer growled softly. "Noted."

Elena smiled, meeting them at the door when they walked inside. "There you are!" she exclaimed, tight hugs for both of them. "I'm pleased to see the both of you."

Matt kissed her cheek and then spotted something intriguing and familiar on the counter—a worn, metal 13x9 cake pan that was older than Matt. "What's this?" He chuckled, a grin on his face as he spotted a familiar dessert. He touched his finger to the whipped topping frosting. "What did he do now?"

Just then he heard Sabrina's voice calling for their grandmother. Elena's eyes narrowed, and she muttered something to herself that Matt didn't understand and walked to the back of the house. Matt continued to laugh.

"I don't get the joke." Sawyer bent over, inspecting the cake. "But that looks good."

"It is." Matt pulled a small plate out of a cabinet. He cut a piece out of the rectangular pan and handed Sawyer a fork. "This is my grandpa's famous *Tres Leches* cake."

"I've heard of it." Sawyer ate a bite and groaned in pleasure. "This is so moist."

"Family recipe," Matt said. "My grandpa adds a little rum in there to spice things up."

"Your grandpa made this, huh." Sawyer followed Matt to the table, taking another bite as they sat down. "I thought your grandma was the chef in the family."

"She is." Matt looked around to see if any of his family were listening. "Grandpa only makes this when he's in the shithouse and wants her to forgive him for something that he did. It's guaranteed to bring the lovers back together again."

Sawyer laughed, throwing his head back as he snickered. "That's awesome. You have the best family." They finished their cake, and Matt quickly washed the plates. "Now I want to know what happened too."

"Hey, brother." Sabrina stepped into the living room as they walked to the bedrooms to unpack their overnight bags. She hugged both of them. "Great to see you guys."

"You too."

Sabrina snorted as Sawyer took his bag into the guest room. "My God, that's adorable." She wrapped her arm around Matt. "Soooo while I've got you here, can you help me with something outside? Please? I need a mechanical engineer, or a plumber... but I guess you'll have to do."

"Of course." Matt tossed his backpack onto his bed, where apparently, he'd be sleeping alone tonight. "When?"

"Whenever you've got time, though the sooner, the better." Sabrina walked into her room and grabbed her jacket off the back of a chair. "Got time right now?"

Sawyer turned to Matt. "Go, do whatever you guys need to do. I'll see if I can help your grandma get set up. Maybe I can catch the entire process from beginning to end."

"That sounds good. I'll wait for you outside." Sabrina waved at Sawyer and walked away.

Matt touched his arm, squeezing it. "You'd better remember what she teaches you, so you can make these for me later."

"So greedy." Sawyer kissed his nose before he walked toward the kitchen.

Matt found a heavier jacket in his room and followed Sabrina outside. "What's wrong?"

"Got a leak in one of the pipes, the one leading out to the cows' automatic waterer. I already turned off the water to that part of the property. It shouldn't be that complicated to fix, but it helps if I've got another set of hands, and you know Grandpa and plumbing."

They strode into the barn, gathering tools and setting them in the back of her four-wheeler, and were soon on their way.

Sabrina pointed out the spot where she suspected the damaged pipe was located, and soon Matt had dug down and uncovered the PVC pipe. "It's like surgery," he said as he cut a section of the cracked pipe while Sabrina measured the new part. They fastened the new pipe with new couplings and Teflon tape, cementing it into place with PVC cement. "We should wait a bit for it to dry and then test it out. Twenty minutes should be enough."

Sabrina put the tools back into their vehicle. "So, how have you been doing?"

Matt grinned, sitting on the ground. "Pretty good. It's been an interesting year so far."

"Looks like it." She joined him on the ground, pushing his knee with her hand. "He sounds like a decent guy."

"He is," Matt admitted, a shy grin on his face.

"And?" Sabrina scooted around to face him. "C'mon, I want details. Tell me what's going on."

Unbelievable. "We've only been dating for a couple of weeks. It's fun, and right now, I'm enjoying it. But I don't know what's going to happen. He's not even from here. Hell, he lives in a house with wheels. I know he'd planned on being in Texas for a while, but he wants to leave eventually. Get back on the open road and travel some more."

"Maybe he didn't have anyone to hang around for." When Matt didn't answer, she continued. "You're allowed to have someone to love in your life. Maybe you should add that column to your stupid spreadsheet."

Matt rolled his eyes at her. "You're assuming a lot, you know."

But she kept talking. "I'm serious. You're a success at work. Everyone thinks you're amazing. But don't get so caught up in being Mister Perfect and afraid of failing that you miss out on a wonderful guy right under your nose."

Matt looked up at her. "You think I'm afraid of failing? "

"Have you met you, Matt? Everything is a contest you have to win, a battle where you have to come out on top."

That was crazy talk. He stood, stretching his legs. "I don't think so."

"Back to what I was saying." Sabrina stood up and looked him square in the face. "Sawyer is easily the hottest man to walk into that shitty little town in years, and he wants you." She nudged him. "He really likes you."

Matt started glancing around the pasture. "That's funny," he replied. "I don't see your significant other around here anywhere." Giving her a pointed look, he squeezed her shoulder. "Or is this a 'do as I say, not as I do' sort of moment?"

She snorted, peeking down at her watch. She rose and made her way toward the four-wheeler. "Point taken. And next time there is a hot guy who's in love with me and I'm ignoring him, feel free to pull me aside and point out how I'm fucking up my life."

"Deal."

"I'll call as soon as I turn on the water." Sabrina drove off in the direction of the water shut-off valve, and a few minutes later, Matt's phone rang. "How's it looking?" she asked.

Matt glanced down at the sealed pipe. "We did it, sis. I'll start filling in the hole. I'll meet you back at the barn."

When Matt and Sabrina entered the kitchen, they saw Sawyer and Elena setting up their assembly line all along the kitchen table. "Okay, what's the story here?" Matt inhaled. The scent of something warm and meaty coming from the stove filled the kitchen. "Can I just get a bowl of whatever that is?"

"No." Elena aimed him toward the kitchen sink. "Go wash your hands. Then get your grandpa and come back and sit down."

They walked to the sink and washed up, and Sabrina went off in search of her grandfather. Matt recognized the corn husks soaking in a bowl next to the sink. "Need this?"

"Yes, bring that. Drain it first." Elena turned her attention back to the stove, where Sawyer stirred an enormous pot. "How does the meat look?"

"Tender," Sawyer said. "Drying out a little bit."

Elena smiled. "That's what we want." Looking back over at Matt, she pointed at a chair at the kitchen table. "Sit." Soon Sabrina and Hector joined them, as Sawyer brought over an enormous bowl filled with a shredded meat in a red sauce and carefully set it down.

"Is that pork?" Matt asked.

Elena nodded. "It is. Sawyer made the Ancho chile sauce." She placed two bowls of masa dough on either side of the table, where they all could reach it more easily. "Alright, here we go." Sitting next to her husband, Elena assembled a tamale for them to see. "You hold the husk in your hand like this, and then spread a little of the masa—not too much." She showed them the thin layer of dough on the husk, then added a little meat and folded in the sides and bottom of the corn husk, revealing a neat little package for all to see. "Okay, get started."

Matt watched as Sawyer made his first tentative tamale, his eyes on Elena's quick, sure hands, trying to emulate her moves. He had trouble folding it, so Matt reached over and held his fingers, demonstrating how to wrap it all up.

As each person finished, they handed their tamale to Elena, who collected them and set them in a large stock pot. When the pot was full, Hector put in on the stove to steam while everyone else continued making the next batch.

A couple of hours later, Hector took the last of the tamales out of the steamer and set them aside to cool.

Sabrina wrapped cooked tamales by the dozen, peering over at the last pot and counting. "We should have almost twelve dozen when we're all done. Not bad for an afternoon's work." She grinned.

"You both will get to take some home." Elena walked toward the sink, where Matt and Sawyer finished washing and drying the dishes. "Thank you, boys," she said, giving each man a hug.

Matt saw Sawyer leaning into that hug. "Thank you. I pick up so much whenever I come visit you. I can't wait to write about this and try to make them myself."

Elena smiled brightly. "You can understand why it's a family activity in our culture. Very labor intensive, but many hands make light work."

Sawyer looked reflective. "My mom always says that. It's true."

Matt watched them with a wide smile; they were both special to him. But when he wiped his hands on his jeans, Elena clucked her displeasure. "Hey, you." Matt shuffled over next to Sawyer. "You wanna go look around?"

"I'd love to." Sawyer's blue eyes sparkled brightly. "Let me get my jacket."

They went out the back door, and for a moment Matt thought about strolling out in the trees or going down by the river where they'd been before. But when he spotted the barn door open, he had another idea.

"What are you doing?" Sawyer asked as they walked inside the barn, Matt sliding the barn door behind him and latching it closed.

"If you insist on sleeping in the guest room," Matt began, sauntering toward Sawyer, "then I thought we could have a little alone time out here."

"Oh my God." Sawyer's eyes grew wide as Matt wound his arms around his waist. "A literal roll in the hay."

"You don't have to roll." Matt tugged him toward an empty horse stall. "You can just lie there."

"That's awful, Mateo." But Sawyer's hands slid under Matt's shirt, lightly scratching his back until Matt shivered. "Cold, baby?"

"I'm good." Matt nuzzled his nose along Sawyer's jaw, fingers ghosting down his body, cupping his bulge through his jeans. "I'm great."

"Awful," Sawyer repeated, then kissed him tenderly. Matt lifted his free hand to Sawyer's hair and tugged at his hair tie until it was free. He loved the feel of Sawyer's hair in his hands.

Stepping backward until his legs hit a soft bundle of hay, Matt pulled back from those soft kisses long enough to reach over and grab an old blanket thrown across the stall. He spread it on a pile of hay bales and lay back on it, tugging Sawyer on top of him.

Sawyer's mouth found Matt's neck, his skin on fire everywhere Sawyer's tongue dragged across his skin. He unzipped Sawyer's pants, laughing as the man worked on his jeans and soon, they were stroking each other, sharing startlingly sweet kisses, oblivious to everyone else in the world, as if all that mattered were the two of them in that barn.

······•••····

Sawyer drew the line at showering together at the ranch, so after dinner he went to wash up and get ready to turn in for the night. Matt sat at the kitchen table, nibbling on popcorn with his laptop open. *Maybe a wallet,* he thought, clicking on a link that led him to a page filled with gifts for men.

"What are you doing?"

"Wha—" Matt glanced up, jumping in his chair as Sabrina touched his arm. "Dammit, you startled me. I'm going to get you a bell to wear around your neck, like a cat. Don't pounce like that."

"Meow." She glanced over his shoulder. "What are you looking at?"

He turned the laptop away from her. "Nothing."

She laughed, turning it back toward her and looking at the words typed into the search box. *Valentine presents for men.* "Aww."

"Stop."

She kissed the top of his head. "This is delightful, Matt. Why are you such a grouch?" She perched next to him, scooting her chair closer. "So, what are you two doing for Valentine's Day?"

"I don't know." When she stared incredulously at him, Matt continued. "We've been dating for a couple of weeks."

"It's been almost a month," Sabrina answered, "and it'll be another couple of weeks by Valentine's Day. You need to get him a present." She nudged him in the belly. "A good one too, for putting up with you."

"Go away."

Sabrina ignored this. "What did you get him for Christmas?" Matt shook his head. "Just as I thought. But he brought you a present, correct?"

Matt smiled to himself. "Cupcake pans. It was a...private joke."

"No, it wasn't a joke. It was a thoughtful gift, cute and intimate. Now you must do the same."

Matt stared at her. "Must I?"

"Yes. What are you considering?"

That was the problem. "I've got no idea," he admitted. "Maybe I should go the funny route, get him something silly, like a gag gift."

Sabrina's face wrinkled in disgust. "Absolutely not."

Matt sighed. "A wallet, maybe?" Sabrina shook her head in disapproval. "Yeah, it's pretty lame. Okay, what else? Maybe something for his kitchen?"

She nodded. "That could be cool. Appropriate. Does he need anything?"

"That's a good question. I don't know."

"Then you need to find out," she told him. "Maybe something related to cooking from Texas. He probably doesn't have equipment like that. Barbecue things or something for Mexican cuisine."

Matt bit his bottom lip, looking over at her. "Do you think getting a person who cooks things connected to cooking is the best decision? It seems the obvious choice."

She narrowed her eyes. "I'm trying to help." She was silent a moment, then blinked. "I got it. Take him on a trip. A getaway weekend, just the two of you. You come here a lot to help us and deserve a little holiday break too."

She wasn't wrong. "What are you thinking?"

"New Orleans," she said without skipping a beat. "It's fun and sexy, and I'll bet he's never been."

Matt snorted. "I've never been there."

"Even better." Sabrina patted him on the shoulder. "Get a nice hotel room in the French Quarter and sit back for a couple of days, eating and drinking. You should go get your tarot cards read. And take one of those riverboat rides." She sighed again. "And eat beignets. Also, you should bring me along, because this sounds like fun."

It was a perfect idea, aside from taking his sister on a romantic weekend with his lover. "I'll consider it."

Sabrina grinned. "I got your back, brother—you know that. I don't know why you don't ask me for help more often."

February

"Mr. Evans!" Matt heard the kids calling out, a couple of them dropping their streamers and running over to the cafeteria doors. Turning, he noticed Sawyer walking in, holding a plastic bag. He finished inflating a pink balloon and tied it off before walking over toward Sawyer, now surrounded by kids.

"Hey there." Sawyer made his way through the small crowd of students who circled him, wanting to talk to him and see what was in the bag. "How are you doing?"

"You guys, all of you get back to work." Matt called them back to their jobs. "Doors open in an hour."

Sawyer offered a few one-armed hugs to a couple students and then looked up at Matt, a silly grin on his face. "Tell me again how you got roped into chaperone duty?" He looked at the balloon in Matt's hand and dropped his voice. "You know you secretly love this shit."

"Ah, yeah, except when I don't." Matt laughed, tossing the balloon at Sawyer. "You left, so it was decided that I have to step in and do it all. Volunteer for everything." He looked at the bag, his eyebrow arched. "What's in there?" Matt held out his hands, only to watch Sawyer pull the bag back, out of his reach. "It's for me, right?"

"Might be," Sawyer said. "What's the magic word?"

Matt leaned in, lowering his voice to a whisper. "Yes." He grinned as Sawyer laughed and handed the bag to him. He pulled out a small plastic bowl and opened the lid, spotting the familiar stew, pork and hominy in a red chile broth. Could it be? "Is this posole?"

"Yeah." Sawyer got out a pouch from his satchel and handed it over to Matt, along with a spoon. "Elena gave me her recipe, walked me through it earlier today. Couldn't let you stuff yourself on pizza and soda tonight." Matt sat down at one of the cafeteria tables, setting the baggie and spoon down next to him. "Spent the morning roasting the ancho chiles and then watched it simmer all afternoon." He reached into the satchel once more and handed Matt a can of flavored carbonated water. "The Airstream smells so good, you can't imagine."

But Matt could. He recalled many chilly evenings coming home late from basketball practice to find his favorite stew simmering in his grandmother's old cast-iron pot. "What's in the baggie?"

"Garnishes," Sawyer answered. "Cilantro, avocado, and a little lime wedge."

Unbelievable. "You're spoiling me." Matt picked up the spoon and tasted it. "This is perfect." At least until he spotted Laverne coming their way. Matt pulled his bowl toward him, possessively. "Get away from me."

To no avail. "I hope you made enough for me too." She laughed, giving Sawyer a hug. "We miss you around here."

Sawyer flushed, grinning as they sat on the opposite side of the table from Matt. "I was over at the elementary school on Monday and Tuesday. Fourth grade," he added. All three of them made a face at that. "But I'll be back next week. I picked up a couple of days for Dorothy, so I'll get to see the kids again."

"Oh, good. It's been too long." Laverne stood, hugging Sawyer once more and then waving at Matt, who'd been steadily eating during this conversation. "You should stay for a couple of hours if you can. The kids'll be thrilled to see you."

Sawyer cocked an eyebrow at Matt. "You mind if I hang out a bit?"

Matt chuckled, wiping his mouth with a napkin. "Go for it. You can blow up those balloons while I eat."

Sawyer stood and gave him a brief salute, then walked toward the helium tank with Laverne. Matt finished the stew and put the container back into the plastic bag, tucking it inside Sawyer's satchel and setting it behind the concession table next to his own backpack.

By the time the dance started, the cafeteria had transformed into a pink-and-red wonderland. Matt had assumed the students would've destroyed the balloons and all his hard work, but half an hour into the festivities, most of them remained intact and unpopped. Matt watched over the concessions with the student council kids, monitoring the money box and making sure no one stole any candy from the table. Every time he looked up, Sawyer was walking around with Dan and Bridget, scanning the crowd and picking up trash. At the one-hour mark, two more parents arrived and took over concession table duty, so Matt waved goodbye to the students and wandered out to see what was happening on the dance floor.

Quite a lot, it seemed. The DJ had a dance contest going, most of the students forming a ring around a couple of kids who were freestyling in the center. Matt felt a tap on his shoulder. He turned and saw Sawyer step up behind him, his satchel slung around his arm.

"Feeling like busting a move, Ruiz?"

"Definitely not," Matt answered with mock solemnity, but the music was loud, much too loud for any kind of discussion. Nodding to the side of the cafeteria, they left the large room and walked down the corridor, the din of the sound system still ringing in his ears. Or maybe the music was that loud. "Are you leaving now?" he asked as they made their way toward the entrance to the school.

"Yeah." Sawyer shifted his satchel from one arm to the other. "I got the truck parked out front."

They exited the building, and Matt could still hear the music playing from the cafeteria. Looking up, he saw a clear sky full of stars. "Thanks for coming. And bringing me dinner. Oh, and helping chaperone. Thanks for everything."

Sawyer looked at him with the softest expression on his face. "Anytime, Ruiz."

Matt's hand fell to the side of his body, his fingers drifting over toward Sawyer's hand, fingertips touching, pinkies linking. Christ, this was dumb. But the sweetest dumb Matt had had in a long fucking time. "I guess the dance was a success. The kids were happy to see you."

"Well, I was glad to help." A soft smile broke across his face. "It was fun watching you too. And I wanted to make sure you ate at a decent hour."

"You mean nine-thirty isn't a decent hour?" Matt asked, and Sawyer groaned at that, slipping his hand slipped around Matt's waist and resting his forehead against Matt's temple. The DJ had put on a slow song and Matt knew he should get back inside and watch for kids making out, but Sawyer swayed with the music and before Matt knew it, they were dancing.

"Come by tonight?" Sawyer whispered into his ear.

"Yeah." Matt looked up at him. "You know, I planned on driving to the ranch this weekend since I haven't been there in a couple of weeks. Lemme run home and grab my laptop, and I'll just leave from your place in the morning." He smiled, feeling Sawyer kissing his cheek. "Why don't you come—"

He heard something, voices, laughter. Turning his head, Matt looked up in the sound's direction. "What was that?" Taking two steps toward the school, he sighted two students with their phones out, recording them. They rushed back into the building, rounding the corner down the hallway and back towards the cafeteria. "Shit."

Sawyer's brows furrowed. "Maybe they didn't—"

But Matt wouldn't let Sawyer say anything further. "Yes, they did. Shit." Matt pushed him away. "This is what I didn't want. This is what I didn't fucking want." Growling, he kicked the curb to the parking lot. "I gotta go fix this."

"Matt." Sawyer took a step forward.

"Don't 'Matt' me." Matt pulled away, pacing. "I told you, I can't do this here. This is my job, my fucking job, do you understand that?"

"Loud and clear. I'm sorry."

"Are you? You get to leave, drive off in your trailer, and I'm the one who's stuck here dealing with the consequences." Sawyer's face froze as if someone had slapped him, but Matt didn't care. "We can't do this."

Sawyer nodded. "You mean tonight, this weekend or...?" When Matt didn't respond, he continued. "Or you mean you and me, we can't do this?"

Matt looked back up at the sky. So many stars. "This is my job, Sawyer."

"Yeah, I got that when you shouted it at me a couple of times." Sawyer folded his hands together. He glanced down, his laugh low and bitter. "I don't know why I'm so fucking surprised. I predicted this. I told you this would happen, remember?" They stood glaring at each other for a long minute until Sawyer looked away, almost in disgust. "Goodbye, Matt."

Matt turned and stormed back inside the dark hallway and into the cafeteria. No one said anything to him about being gone.

"Everything alright?" Laverne asked, two empty soda cans in her hands. "You look upset, hon."

He shook his head and spent the rest of the evening by himself. His expression kept everyone away.

He heard his phone go off a few times that night, but he ignored it.

· · · · ● · · ● · · ·

Early the next morning, Matt tossed his clothes into a bag, packed up his laptop, and drove out toward the ranch. He spotted Sabrina in the barn as he pulled up next to her car. She waved at him, then pointed at their ancient John Deere tractor and made a thumbs-down motion with her hand. He waved back and nodded, then walked inside.

His grandmother wasn't in the kitchen. "Hello," he called out, not spotting her.

"Over here," she answered and, following the sound of her voice, Matt found her in her bedroom, sitting in her closet. Boxes and piles of clothes covered her bed. "Hi, *mijo*. I'm so glad to see you." Before Matt could respond, she added, "Can you hand me that?" Elena stood and pointed at a shelf high above her head. He pulled down a cardboard box and set it on the ground. "Thank you." She kissed his cheek. "Hungry?"

"Not really," Matt told her, but he followed her into the kitchen and sat at the table, accepting a cup of coffee and coffee cake. "Sit down with me. What are you doing in your closet?"

Elena cut a piece of coffee cake for herself and joined him. "Going through all those old clothes and the boxes up on top," she answered. "I told your grandpa we needed to get rid of all our junk. You and Sabrina shouldn't be going through all our things once we're gone."

"Don't talk like that." Matt took a sip from his cup. "You're not going anywhere."

She laughed. "Do you want to go through those boxes of Beanie Babies after I'm dead?" Elena reached out and took his hands in hers. "We're not getting younger. But if it makes you feel better, you can imagine I'm just spring cleaning my bedroom."

He snorted, but felt her eyes on him, looking at him. Really looking.

"What's wrong?" she asked. "You look like you aren't sleeping."

It had taken a while to fall asleep the night before, but Matt didn't realize he looked tired. "Nothing. Just... I've been busy. Lots going on at work and school."

She smiled at him, reaching out and messing with his hair. "I'm glad you're here then. You can rest and sleep in late tomorrow. Maybe later you can set up your computer over here on the kitchen table, and I'll help you with your homework like I used to when you were little."

Matt laughed at that. "Sounds good." He finished his snack in two more bites. "What's going on in the barn?"

Elena grumbled, and her face darkened as she stood. She took the plates over to the sink. "That damn tractor. It hasn't run in years and all of a sudden, he wants to get it started. I wish he'd get rid of it." She brought the coffee pot over and refilled her cup. "Maybe he'll listen to you."

Later that afternoon, Matt bit the bullet and began going through the messages on his phone.

> Cora: *What happened?*
>
> Laverne: *It's not that bad. It's really not that bad.*
>
> Alicia: *Call me if you need to talk. Don't get all upset over this.*
>
> Cora: *Hey I don't know if you saw this. Call me.*

Shit.

His heart raced as he realized someone had uploaded a video on YouTube, and with a shaking hand he clicked on the link. They titled the video "My Gay Teachers." It looked like a cell phone camera zooming in on him and Sawyer talking in the parking lot. All the air whooshed out of Matt's lungs as he saw their hands tangled, Sawyer leaning in and kissing him, and the two of them dancing. Fuck, what had he been expecting? They'd been fucking dancing in the parking lot of his middle school.

They added a cheesy love song to play during this video. And there were comments, of course there were comments.

LOL05: I didn't know they were dating!

monfreya: Boyfriends!

iamasquid: Gross.

k1tty12: Ah I love them! They're so cute together!

_off_jacked: Fags.

HiBiKaBa: I ship them hard.

Fuck. *Fuck, fuck, fuck.* Matt tossed the phone back on his bed and held his head in his hands. This was exactly what he'd worked so hard to avoid, being that teacher. The gay teacher. The fag teacher.

And Sawyer, dammit, of course he didn't understand. Another couple of months, and he'd have moved on from this town. This wasn't going to haunt Sawyer for years to come. But for Matt, the video would blow up each fall when school began, and again each February when the dance rolled around, and the video was shared with all his new students. It could be life-altering for him, potentially career-ending, and Matt couldn't comprehend why everyone was telling him it wasn't a big deal.

Dinner that night was quiet.

"How's your friend?" Sabrina asked, teasing as she speared her asparagus. "I'd hoped you might bring him here this weekend." She grinned at her grandmother. "I told Grandma to make up the guest room."

"Don't tease your brother." Elena added more roast chicken onto her plate. "How did the posole turn out?" When Matt didn't answer, Elena put her fork down. "Mateo, what's wrong?"

Matt went still. "Nothing. It's just... We're not... I don't think we'll be seeing much of each other anymore."

Silence filled the room. "Did you have a fight?" Sabrina asked. "What did you do?"

Matt's face darkened. "Don't."

Hector gave her a sharp look, then turned to Matt. "Don't worry about it. You don't have to talk about it if you don't want to." A few more uncomfortable minutes passed before Matt excused himself. He could hear them continuing their conversation as he marched into the living room, dropping onto the sofa and turning on the television.

Later that night, Sabrina walked out of her room in her pajamas and joined him on the sofa. "What happened?" When Matt didn't answer, she reached over and grabbed the remote control from his lap and paused the show.

"Dammit," Matt said. "Leave me alone."

"No. Tell me what happened, and I'll leave you alone." She reached for his hand. "But you're telling me first."

They stared at each other for a minute before Matt gave up. Reaching for his cell phone, he scrolled through his messages to the one that had the link to the video and handed it to her. He heard the song play again, that silly, stupid song about love and forever, and he pictured that video in his head, the two of them touching, kissing, dancing...

"Oh." Sabrina sighed. "What— When was this?"

"Last night." Matt took his phone back and set it on the table. "Valentine's dance at school."

She reached out and stroked his arm. "He really likes you. Anyone with eyes can see that."

"Maybe. Doesn't matter anymore."

"Doesn't it?" she asked. "This isn't—"

"Don't tell me it's not a big deal. What is my boss going to say? What are the coaches going to say? What about the parents of my students?" he asked, his voice rising.

Sabrina glared back at him. "They're going to be thrilled you finally found someone to love, you prickly bastard." They stared at each other more until she smiled, reaching over and hugging him. "I'm sorry, big brother. You know I want you to be happy."

"Yeah." Matt nodded. For all they grumbled, Matt knew his sister loved him. "Maybe one of these days. But now...now's not a good time."

· · · • · • · • · · ·

"Hey, Rosa."

"Hi, Matt." The principal's secretary glanced up at him and smiled. "How're you doing today?" She tilted her head up as she studied at him from behind her computer.

"Not too bad. Is he in there?" Matt pointed at Curt's closed door and rocked on the balls of his feet.

"Pretty sure, go on over and check."

Matt tried to tell himself the sympathetic look she gave him was coincidental, that everybody at the school wasn't chatting about him and Sawyer. The dance had been Friday night, and while none of the kids he'd taught all day had mentioned anything directly to him, he saw it in their faces. Or was he imagining it? Matt erred on the side of caution. Or paranoia, that's what Cora had called it. "Hey," he said, knocking on the principal's door, his stomach in knots. "You asked to see me?"

"Yeah, come on in." Curtis didn't stand, but pointed to the chair in front of his desk. Matt, overcome by a strong sense of déjà vu, sat down and exhaled slowly. "How have you been doing today?"

"I'm okay." Matt shrugged. "Feel a little like I'm jumping at shadows."

Curtis nodded. "Nothing worse than being the object of office gossip. Anyone making you feel uncomfortable about what took place? Asking you a lot of questions about it?"

Matt shook his head. "No, no one's mentioned it. At least, not here at work. I've talked about it with a couple of friends this weekend." Matt folded his hands in front of him. "I need to apologize. Um, that shouldn't have happened, not at school, and not anywhere where someone could record a video. I profoundly regret it and will take whatever steps needed to make it right."

"Matt." Curtis leaned forward on his desk. "First, I need you to understand I'd be having this discussion if this were a... heterosexual couple. None of this—" he pointed between the two of them, "—we're not meeting here because you're gay. I'm aware what kind of man you are, how strong that sense of propriety runs in you. This was embarrassing for you, and I'm sorry. Rebecca spoke with the girl who recorded the video this morning. She says it was not her intention to embarrass you; they thought it was 'a cute moment,' I guess," he said, glancing over at a handwritten statement on his desk. Matt presumed it was the student in question. "We've asked her to remove the video, and Ms. Hogan called her parents earlier today and let them know we communicated with their daughter and what it was about."

Matt felt all the air leave his lungs. The girl was in his second period class. "I wish you hadn't—"

"Again," Curtis said. "If they'd uploaded any recording of my teachers, we'd be talking to the student and calling home. They're not allowed to do that, no matter how innocent their intentions." He paused for a moment. "Do you have any questions?"

"Do I need to do anything? Sign anything?" Matt looked around for some sort of reprimand slip, official documentation that they'd spoken to him.

"Dammit, Matt. Am I allowed to kiss my wife in front of the school?" Curtis asked with more than a hint of exasperation in his tone.

Matt looked him straight in the eye. "You're not gay."

"And you're not in trouble." Curtis looked at him sympathetically. "Having said that, I'd avoid situations that might leave you vulnerable to this sort of scrutiny—gay, straight, or otherwise."

"That's not a problem." Matt stood, taking a deep breath. "There won't be anything like that happening ever again."

March

Missing Sawyer wasn't something on Matt's endless list of things to do, and yet here he was, lying in bed and wasting time thinking about his ex-boyfriend. But he needed to get up, so he swung his legs over the side of his bed and sat there another moment. He'd never understood the term "heartache" before, but now he sat up, rubbing his chest as if it would make the physical ache in his body stop.

It didn't.

Keeping busy helped during the day, but at night, Matt missed those long arms around him, their feet tangling together playfully. Mornings were hard too, those fuzzy moments before he woke up, before he remembered they didn't love each other anymore.

•••••••••••

"Hey, Grandma, sorry to call so late. The track meet ran long."

"It's fine, don't worry. Your grandpa's out in the garden and I'm sitting on the porch watching him. It's getting warmer at night, and it's beautiful outside right now." Matt agreed. Spring had hit early this year. "Did your school win?" she asked.

"No, we didn't win this time, but the girls did fantastic." He paused as sat on the edge of his bed and pulled off his boots as she talked on. "Grandpa wants what? How many are 'a few more cows'?"

"Exactly. That's what I want to know."

Matt ran a hand over his face. "No, I get it. Um, let me talk to him next time I come down."

"Are you off from school yet?" she asked.

"Yeah, today was the last day but I'm not going to the ranch for spring break. You remember I told you about starting a Robotics Club at my school? Anyway, there's a big competition in San Antonio over spring break, and I'm taking some of my kids."

"You're taking them to San Antonio for the week?"

"No, just a couple of days. We'll drive up and back each day. But maybe I can go out to the ranch the weekend after." He lay back on his bed, staring up at the ceiling. "Let me see how much homework I can get done before—"

"Don't worry about it if you've got things to do. We love you."

"No, no, it's fine." Pausing, he reached over and grabbed his laptop from next to his bed. "I love you too. Tell everyone there I said hello and I'll see you all soon."

After hanging up with his grandmother, Matt opened a browser and found Sawyer's YouTube channel. He hadn't watched any of them since they'd broken up, but Cora had mentioned to him that the latest video was up, and it featured Elena teaching Sawyer how to make tortillas. Matt clicked the link, unable to keep the smile off his face as he saw them cooking together in that familiar kitchen. Her grandmother looked so small next to him, but they both laughed as they rolled out the dough and then tasted their tortillas, warm with butter.

Scrolling down, he saw his name in the notes below the video. *Much love and thanks to Elena and Hector Navarro, Sabrina Ruiz, and Matt Ruiz at the Rancho Rio Riendo for their hospitality and friendship.*

Well. That didn't hurt.

• • • • • • • • • •

They held the state robotics competition in San Antonio that year, close enough that they could drive into the city each morning of the competition and still be home before it got dark. For two days, Matt carpooled with his students and their parents up to the big convention center, where they watched students from across the state compete against each other with robots they'd designed and built. They saw robots of all sizes carrying out all sorts of tasks and competing for prizes, and Matt and his students left each day with equipment and ideas for projects they wanted to try with their own club the following next year.

Each day, he passed Sawyer's RV park as they left town and then returned. Sometimes the truck was there. Other times it wasn't.

All Matt could think about was sharing this with Sawyer. It had been Sawyer's idea, and twice he almost picked up his phone to tell Sawyer how much the kids loved it when it hit him again, like a hammer. It was over. They were over.

••••••••••

After spring break, the year picked up speed. Track and field wasn't his favorite sport, but it kept him busy after school, the track meets taking up a lot of his time on weekends. He saw Sawyer less and less at school, guessing that he was only substituting once every couple of weeks. When they saw each other, they didn't speak.

The days ran into each other, one after the other, and despite the bluebonnets and other bright spring flowers popping up along the highways, Matt's world was colorless, and no matter how busy he kept himself, it all felt empty.

It was a sunny spring afternoon when Matt pulled into his driveway, noticing Cora's small Toyota Camry parked in front of his house. She sat on his doorstep. "Hey, stranger." She stood, sizing him up. "Can we talk?"

As if he had a choice. Matt nodded, then opened the door. "Want something to drink?"

"Whatever you've got." They sat at the kitchen table with a couple of bottles of lemonade. "First, I'm sorry for invading your space like this, but you've been avoiding me for weeks now and I needed to talk to you about what happened."

Fuck. Matt shook his head. "It doesn't matter anymore. I didn't get into trouble, and now I want to forget it."

"I'm not talking about the dance." Cora tapped a finger on the table. "I mean, what happened with the relationship. You and Sawyer. You know he misses you."

"He's doing fine without me." Matt had watched Sawyer's latest video, this one from a Houston soul food restaurant, a mystery person holding the camera as he described the food. "This was never supposed to be forever, Cora. It was always going to end when he moved on." He took a sip from his drink. "People move on. That's what they do."

Cora blinked, her eyes narrowing. "Is that what this is about?"

"What do you mean?"

"Matt, are you talking about Sawyer leaving you, or are you speaking about someone else?"

He stiffened in his chair. "Wow, didn't realize you were a psychoanalyst now," he said, his tone chillier than before.

Cora ignored the change in his demeanor. "I'm a teacher, so of course I'm a psychoanalyst. Had you even made that connection yet, that you don't let people get close to you because of what happened to you as a child? It makes perfect sense. I mean, Matt, honey, you still haven't even left home. It's like this bizarre, prolonged adolescence, worried you're doing to be abandoned again."

"Stop." He gripped his bottle. This was getting extremely personal. "Please." Cora didn't speak. They sat in silence for a minute while Matt processed her words. After a minute, he sighed. "Sabrina says I have a fear of failure. I have to be the best."

"It's possible. She would know." Cora looked down at her phone. "But we'll have to discuss that at the next appointment. I'm afraid your time is up for today." They both chuckled, and she leaned over and hugged him. "I miss seeing your face at lunch every day."

"Me too."

April

Matt's thirtieth birthday fell on a Wednesday, and the lunch bunch brought him a cake to celebrate. Deanna beat him to school that morning and decorated his door with streamers and a sign that read "Happy birthday!" All day long, Matt's students asked him how old he was now, and all day he told them the answer.

As the day wore on, he became less amused by their horror at how ancient he was, as if they expected him to fall over any moment.

Even worse, Matt kept checking his phone. He didn't want to admit he'd hoped Sawyer would call or text. It should've been a good day, and yet, he went to bed that evening disappointed with no idea how he was going to fix this.

••••••••••

Easter snuck up on Matt, and before he knew it, the three-day holiday was upon him. "Okay, class, remember that we don't have school tomorrow." He stood in front of his last period of the day. "So that means you have an extra day to finish your homework."

"But I'm gonna be busy on Sunday," Orlando, one of his class clowns, announced.

Matt was in a good mood, so he played along. "Do you have plans with the Easter bunny?"

"Yeah, my grandma still hides eggs for me. Then we hit a *piñata*." He smiled, looking around at his classmates. "Last year I got ten dollars and a bag of chocolate."

The class laughed, and as the bell rang, Matt dismissed them, shaking his head and walking back to his desk. "Be safe and have a great weekend."

"You doing anything, Mr. Ruiz?" Orlando asked, as he walked by.

"Yeah, I'm going to see my grandparents as well."

Orlando smiled. "Your grandma still hides eggs for you too?"

"She might." Matt grinned at his student. "Have fun."

Matt packed what he needed for the weekend and drove out to the ranch, arriving as the sun was going down. "Need any help?" he asked, spotting his grandfather and Sabrina leaving the barn.

"We're good." Sabrina danced around the dogs, who ran straight for Matt. He greeted them, then joined the others as they walked into the house. "How are you doing?"

"I've got a paper to finish, but that's it for the weekend." Truth be told, he hadn't even started it yet. This week had been hard for Matt to concentrate on his studies. Every night when he got home, he sat in front of his computer and found a hundred other things to look at. For the first time since he'd started his classes, he wasn't earning full points for his assignments, and his grades had dropped.

Sabrina offered to take Elena to the grocery store on Saturday morning, so Matt joined his grandfather and helped feed the cows. He tossed a bag of cow supplemental pellets onto the back of his truck and climbed into the driver's seat.

They made their way toward the far pasture in silence.

"What's wrong?" Hector asked when a few minutes went by with no conversation.

Matt shook his head. "Just feeling a little low, Grandpa. It's been a rough month."

"Got kicked in the *cojones*?"

Matt snorted at that. "Yeah. I don't know, maybe I did it to myself." He recalled what Cora and Sabrina had told him. "Do you think I have a fear of failure?"

Hector didn't speak for a moment, and when he did, it surprised Matt. "Yes. You've always concerned yourself too much with what other people think. Always too worried."

"But lots of people are like that."

"To some extent," Hector agreed. "At a certain point, most either stop caring or learn to hide it better. You have that worry right there on the surface."

Well, fuck. Matt hung his head, trying to keep his emotions in check. "Why am I like this?"

Hector pulled up into the pasture and turned off the engine. It was a minute before he spoke. "I used to think it had to do with your mother leaving. Sabrina, she was still so young, she never knew your mom, not really." He looked over at Matt, his eyes dark and sad. "But you remember her, when we all lived together." Matt realized at some point that his grandfather wasn't speaking to his grandson. No, now this was Hector talking to Mateo, man to man. "Elizabeth was never the same after your father went away. She loved you and your sister, but her head..." Hector touched his own forehead with one finger. "She let it get to her up here, and that's all that mattered to her. Being left behind, being abandoned." He snorted. "And then she did the same thing to you two. It was shameful, and I'll never forgive her for that."

"I'm sorry about all of that."

"None of that was your fault," Hector said, anger in his voice. "Never apologize for her. She knew what she did, and that's why she's too ashamed to come crawling back now. And David, your father, never a word to see how his children turned out." Hector's eyes flashed, a side to him Matt rarely saw. "So yes, you always needed to be the best, the smartest, the hardest working. I used to think maybe you tried so hard because she left you, or you wanted your grandma and me to be even more proud of you than we were."

Matt gripped the wheel. "And now?"

"Do you know why you make us so proud? It's not because of your job or your college classes, or your plans for the future. It's because when I asked you to help me this morning, you didn't blink an eye. You didn't ask what it was, you just got up and got ready to help me. You have a loving heart and you're the best son a man could've asked for."

Matt blinked fast, feeling his eyes moisten. "Thanks, Grandpa."

"De nada, Mateo. But don't live your life alone. All your fancy plans mean nothing if you can't share your successes with someone." He stepped out of the vehicle as the cows wandered toward them, knowing food was close by. "And when you mess up, admit your mistakes. There's no shame in failing. That's how we learn, when we mess it up. But say you are sorry." He looked over at the ranch and smiled. "I almost lost your grandma once, when I was young and dumb, because of my pride. If you're wrong, fix it. No one else will."

They dropped scoopfuls of the cow feed on the ground. Hector walked over to the animals and checked on each one, stroking their faces and quietly talking to them in Spanish.

Once he was done, they got back into Matt's truck. "Now, tell me how your track team is doing," Hector said as they drove to the barn. "I want to hear all about it."

· · · • • · • · · ·

Sawyer had posted two new videos, one from Driftwood at a famous barbecue place, and another from Port Aransas, where he fished off a boat and cooked a meal right on the beach. Matt couldn't tell who was operating the camera, and he spent a sleepless night speculating about that mystery person.

· · · • • · • · · ·

"So, look at number seven." Matt pointed at his notes projected on the whiteboard. "A function can have only one output for each input. One Y value for each X value." Silence. "If I'm answering number seven, which one of these tables shows a function?" He walked over to the projector and replaced his notes with the problem, displaying three input/output tables. "How do I solve it? What is the first step?" he asked, looking at his class. But their attention was focused on the door. He turned his head and saw Rebecca Hogan, their vice principal, standing outside in the hall.

She opened the door and walked inside. "Mr. Ruiz, can I speak with you a moment?" Her face was a calm mask that told him something was wrong.

"Of course." She stepped back into the hallway, and he followed, one foot inside his door so he could monitor the class. "Is everything okay?"

"Um, you need to call your sister. I'm here to watch your class while you go. You can use my office if you need some privacy."

This was it. "Is it my grandmother?" he asked point blank, that moment he'd been dreading for years finally here.

"Go call Sabrina," she replied, her voice tight, and Matt knew he was right.

"Um, okay. I'll be back in a few minutes."

"Take as much time as you need."

Matt stepped into the room and picked up his phone. "Class, um, I'll be right back." He pointed to the lesson they were working on and then reminded his students they had to finish their assignment for homework if they didn't complete it before the class ended. *I'm stalling*, he realized, looking at their faces and then again at Rebecca. Finally, he took a breath and headed into the hallways and down the stairs, walking into the front office. Rosa wasn't at her desk, but Matt saw Rebecca's office was empty.

He stepped inside and closed the door. Matt fingered his phone for a moment before he made the call.

"Hey." Sabrina's voice was flat.

Matt swallowed. "What happened?" She'd been fine at Easter, but who knew how this all worked? Had it come back, and she hadn't told them? Was it something different? "Is she okay?"

"Matt." He heard her crying now, her voice breaking as she spoke. "It's Grandpa."

No. Sharp, like a punch to his gut. "Grandpa?" he repeated. "What... How—"

"They think it was a heart attack. I found him this morning, out in the cow pasture." She sniffed. "He went to feed them and when he didn't come back, I walked out there and—" Matt heard her taking deep breaths.

"Where are you?"

"San Pedro Medical Center. The ambulance brought him in, but he wasn't breathing. Grandma's with him right now. Can you come?"

"Yeah, I'm on my way. Hey." Matt imagined what it must have been like for her that morning, finding him out there. "Love you, sister."

She began crying again. "Love you, brother."

Matt arrived at the hospital and spoke with the doctor who'd seen Hector. Sudden cardiac arrest brought about by a massive heart attack. They'd done chest compressions in the ambulance on the way to the hospital, but he was gone by the time they'd arrived. Now, a couple of hours later, Elena held Matt's hand as they sat together in the room with Hector's body.

Sabrina walked back into the room. "I called Miller and Sons Funeral Home. They'll come pick him up tonight."

Elena nodded, looking older and tired. "We made all our arrangements a few years ago, back when I was sick. The funeral home knows what to do. They'll take care of everything." Squeezing Matt's hand, she leaned against his shoulder. "I always thought I'd go first."

"C'mon, Grandma." Matt hugged her. "Let's go home." He couldn't remember feeling this empty, but his first concerns right now were his grandmother and Sabrina. He had to be strong for them.

Elena stood, walking over to Hector. "Can I have a moment with him?"

Matt went over and kissed his grandfather one last time. Sabrina stood next to him. She touched her grandfather's hair and leaned down to kiss his hand. "We'll be outside whenever you're ready," he told his grandmother, as he and Sabrina left the room.

· · · • • · • • · ·

The house was quiet when they walked inside later that afternoon. Matt had stopped off at his house to grab clothes and his laptop before driving back to the ranch. Now he sat in the kitchen and worked on a lesson plan for the rest of the week. He didn't know how long he'd be out, but it made sense to be prepared, just in case.

After emailing Deanna with attachments and instructions for his students, he closed the computer and looked out the kitchen window. There was an assignment for his Specialized Programs class due on Wednesday, but that was two days away. He couldn't concentrate on anything right now but the garden, his grandfather's beautiful green garden. Standing, he went outside, walking through the yard and into the garden.

It was early in the growing season but already there were tomatoes on a few plants, the kale from last year still aggressively taking over their raised bed. Young plants, tucked in their own sections but not labeled. Matt laughed, quiet at first, but soon louder, until a few tears rolled down his cheeks. He didn't know what his grandfather had planted, and probably wouldn't, until they grew and flowered and the vegetables made themselves known.

He was watering the plants with a garden hose when he heard the door open and close. Sabrina set down two bowls of dog food, petting Pancho as he bounded toward her on his way to the bowl. She walked toward Matt and sat down on the grass outside the raised beds. "You okay?"

It was a moment before he answered. "I think I'm still in shock."

"Me too." She pulled a few pieces of grass. "I didn't think it would be him, and yet in retrospect—" she shrugged, "—I don't know why it never occurred to me."

"I don't think I ever saw him sick a day in his life."

"Me neither. I remember when he broke his arm, falling off that ladder." Both of them chuckled, recalling that infamous family story of Hector insisting on removing the satellite dish on their roof, only to end up with a fracture and Elena's worry-flavored wrath.

"How's Grandma?"

"She's okay. Been on the phone all afternoon, telling people not to come over. Later this week, she said, but she only wanted to be with us tonight."

Matt put the hose down, turning off the water. "Did she get a hold of Mom?"

"I don't know."

Matt hoped she didn't. "What's next?"

Sabrina pulled out her phone, sliding her finger on the screen before reading. "We need a death certificate. Funeral home will take care of that. Grandma was right, they'd made all the arrangements when she was sick. Paid for all of it too." She bit her lip and took a deep breath. "Just like him, to make sure we didn't have to worry about any of it." Looking down at her screen, she summarized a text message for him. "They'll call tomorrow to talk about a viewing, if we want one, and a service. Um, they both wanted to be cremated." The dogs finished eating and ran over to where she was sitting. Sabrina began stroking Lefty's fur, Pancho settling next to her on the grass. "Grandma wants his ashes brought back here." Matt heard the tears before he saw them. "She wants to put him out by the big oak, with their Eddie."

· · · • · • · · · ·

Matt ended up taking the entire week off work so he could help his grandmother and sister with funeral preparations. On Tuesday, he drove them into town to go over the arrangements and get copies of the death certificate. Just as Elena had told them, they'd arranged for a simple funeral mass with as little fuss as possible. Matt and Sabrina talked Elena into adding a small lunch after the service in the hall next door to the church to keep people from coming back to the ranch afterward.

After that, they went to see the Navarro's lawyer. "We made all of our plans years ago," Elena reminded them. "We didn't want anyone to worry about this."

"It's surprising how many people don't take the time to make these plans." Angela Rosales, their lawyer, agreed and explained how their arrangements were being settled. They'd left everything to the surviving spouse—in this case, Elena. Hector also had some private bequests, money and personal effects for Sabrina and Matt and a donation to the cancer hospital in Houston where Elena had received her medical treatment. The lawyer ensured she'd make the necessary changes to Elena's paperwork, changing the beneficiaries to Matt and Sabrina now that Hector was gone.

They went out and had lunch while they were in town. "Thank you for both coming with me today," Elena said after they ordered. "I want you both to know what the plans are, no surprises or unpleasantness. Mateo, Sabrina." She reached for each of their hands. "When we first wrote out the will, we weren't sure what was going to happen with you two. At first we assumed you'd both grow up and move away to one of the bigger cities to start your lives." She smiled at Sabrina. "Nothing made your grandpa happier than seeing you grow into a rancher, *mija*. He loved sharing that love of the land with you." Sabrina wiped her eyes with her napkin, and even Matt sniffed a couple of times. But Elena remained clear-eyed, now turning toward Matt. "We always knew you had plans outside Estella, Mateo. We are so proud of you and whatever you did, and we both knew what you gave up staying here close to us." She looked between them. "When I go, the ranch and everything on it goes to both of you, in both your names. You can decide to leave it like that, come to an arrangement, or you can sell it and split the money. Or split the land. Whatever you both want to do. The selfish part of me hopes that one of you stays there, and that the property stays in our family for a little longer."

"It will, Grandma." Sabrina nodded, looking over at Matt and smiling back at her. "I promise."

After they got home, Matt sat in his room and opened his laptop to get his discussion posts written and submitted. Checking his work email, he noticed a high number of unread emails. Suddenly worried, he glanced over at them and realized they were from his coworkers and even a couple of students, offering support and condolences. Matt spent a few minutes answering these and then began working on his assignment.

Later that night, Matt found Sabrina in the kitchen, reading something off her laptop and eating brownies a neighbor had dropped off the previous day. "Hey." He opened the fridge and pulled out a carton of milk. After pouring a glass, Matt joined her at the table. "What's that?" he asked, reaching for a brownie and a napkin.

"Just a few ideas for the ranch. Things I've been kicking around in my head." She turned the screen around so he could see the webpage.

"Chicken coops?" The idea surprised Matt, but it made sense. "So, you're planning on keeping this all going?" Matt leaned back in his chair and faced Sabrina. "We could sell it, you know, get a lot of money for it. Set you and Grandma up in a nice house wherever you want. You guys could come live near me." Their property was beautifully situated, and people were already making inquiries to see if the family was interested in selling part or all of the land.

But Sabrina shook her head. "I want to give this a try for a few years, and see if I can make this place a real moneymaker."

The idea intrigued Matt. "What are you thinking?"

She leaned in. "We'd been talking about selling the cows for a while now. They're not much of an investment for us anymore. Once in a while, he'd talk about getting more, breeding them again, but..." Sabrina shrugged. "We never got around to it. Grandpa stopped selling them like we should have." She laughed softly. "They were more like his pets. He even kept putting off butchering them because he liked to go out and feed them, talk to them."

"He loved them. So, what's this about?" he asked, pointing at the laptop.

"I've been looking into the chicken idea Sawyer mentioned. Fresh eggs are big money at farmer's markets. Just need to make chicken coops and buy a few layers to get started. I think that's what they're called. With a proper investment, selling eggs could bring in a fresh stream of income, especially if we got into the whole farmer's market business, or selling to co-ops. We could turn this ranch into a proper business. Turn a profit instead of just getting by."

Matt was impressed by all of this. "What can I do to help you out?"

Sabrina looked over at him, nodding. "I'll let you know. I might call you to come help sometimes. You can help me build coops, for one. Keeping the land cleaned up." She looked outside the windows. "I'm going to miss seeing him in the garden every morning. I don't have that magical green thumb."

Neither spoke for a moment. "You'll be great at this." Matt couldn't remember being prouder of her. "I'll support whatever decisions you and Grandma make. You're running the show now, sister," he said, resting his hand on hers.

"Thanks, big brother." Sabrina hugged him back. "Love you lots."

"Back at you."

She smiled grimly, but squeezed his hand. "How are things with Sawyer?"

Matt cleared his throat. "He's good, I guess. We don't talk much. I haven't seen him around the school."

"I'm sad to hear that."

"It didn't end well." Matt shrugged, making a face. "That was my fault. I was awful."

"Oh, Matt." Sabrina sighed. "I wish things had worked out for you two."

"I know. But he was right, I'm not the type of person who can let go and be happy with what I have."

"That's a load of bullshit. You deserve to be happy too. The only one keeping that from happening is you."

• • • • • • • • • •

The next day, Matt worked on a slide show for the service. Elena brought out old photo albums to add to the more recent photos he and Sabrina had on their computers. "Look at this," she said, selecting one from Hector's childhood, a black-and-white photograph of a little boy playing in a pile of leaves. "I'd recognize that smile anywhere."

There were other great photos—grade school pictures, high school graduation, photos of Hector and Elena first starting out.

"How old were you here?" he asked, pointing at a picture of her in a short skirt and coiffed hair, Hector wearing bright red corduroy pants and a matching jean jacket.

She looked at it for a long moment. "Eighteen? Maybe nineteen? Elizabeth hadn't been born yet." Matt had heard the story many times, of headstrong, young Hector Ruiz who'd come to town to work in the oil fields and had fallen in love with a rancher's daughter. "Fifty years we had together."

Matt exhaled. "That's incredible." He lifted another photo, seeing his mother as a child. Page after page of a happy family, loving each other. "Seems impossible now for two people to stay together that long."

"Mijo, there's time for you. Don't rush it." Elena reached for his hand. "But don't push it away either, when love presents itself."

Matt looked down. "Did Sabrina tell you what happened?"

She made a soft sound. "Your face told me, Mateo." She touched his cheek, and he closed his eyes. "I've known you since before you were born, and you've never had a secret I didn't know first."

He chuckled, casting his eyes down. "That obvious?"

"To me? Yes. Always." She leaned in and kissed him, then passed him another picture.

"How did you know Grandpa was the one for you?"

Elena stared at the picture. The faded colors couldn't keep the love and laughter from exploding from the image. "There isn't such a thing as just one person for you. Love is all about making another person happy, that joy you feel in here." She touched his chest gently. "When you see that person smile. There will be many people in your life who you'll want to make happy. Once in a while, you meet someone who wants to make you happy too. You fit together like the puzzle pieces, and you just know." She gave his arm a squeeze. "That's the magic, when it happens to both of you at the same time."

Matt remembered that weekend Sawyer had spent at his place, the expression on Sawyer's face when Matt had eaten the lasagna he'd made. "Sometimes I think I'm too selfish to fall in love."

"I hope not," Elena said, "because you're a wonderful man, and I want you to be happy, like your grandpa and I were. I want you to spend fifty years with someone you love."

· · · • • • • • · · ·

Born on August 10, 1943, Hector Navarro was preceded in death by his parents, Jose and Beatriz Navarro, a son, Edward Navarro, and his brother, Lionel Navarro. He is survived by his beloved wife, Elena Navarro, his daughter, Elizabeth Navarro, and two grandchildren, Mateo Ruiz and Sabrina Ruiz. Services will be held Friday morning at Our Lady of Grace Catholic Church at ten o'clock.

Matt was up early on Friday morning. He'd taken on feeding the cows that week to help Sabrina out, and as he drove out to the pasture where they grazed, his grandmother's words floated through his head. Spending a lifetime with another human being. That wasn't anywhere in his timeline, his spreadsheet, his plan for the future. A year ago, Matt wouldn't have given it much thought, wouldn't have been worried about finding another person to spend his life with. If it happened, it happened, but not anytime soon, please.

But today, Matt wasn't so certain. Sure, there was nothing wrong with being alone if that's how the cards played out, but did he want to push away someone who might love him? Did he want to be alone?

Would he come to the end of his time here and have no one who missed him? No family, no great love of his life? Looking back at the ranch, he knew Sabrina would do an outstanding job running the place. It would always be his home, but his grandpa's death left an emptiness that would never be filled.

· · · • • • • • · · ·

Almost two hundred people crowded the pews of Our Lady of Grace Church on Friday morning to attend the funeral service for Hector Navarro. It didn't surprise Matt to see his principal and assistant principal among the mourners, but the number of teachers and coworkers who also attended shocked him. There would be lots of substitutes at Hays Middle School today; Sawyer might be one of them. But just then, he spotted that familiar lanky frame standing next to Cora. Their eyes met, Sawyer offering a sad smile. Matt lifted his hand and waved.

After the service, the guests walked into a reception hall next to the church and had lunch, finger sandwiches and pasta salad. Matt walked around all the tables and spoke to everyone he could. Spotting his coworkers, he went to their table. "Thank you for coming," he told them in a low voice, surprised by the emotion. "It means a lot to me and my family."

"We're thinking about you." Curtis reached out and touched his arm. "Take care of your family and let us know if you need anything."

"I think we're about done with everything." That evening, they'd bury Hector's ashes back on the property. "I should be back at school on Monday." Several of them stood, getting ready to leave and get back to work. Cora and Sawyer walked toward him. "Thanks for being here," Matt said as Cora's arms circled him, hugging him tight.

"I'm so sorry, Matt. He was a great man."

"He was." Matt turned toward Sawyer. "Hi."

Sawyer smiled at him, but it was bittersweet, tinged with sadness. "I'm so sorry, Matt. I didn't know him well, but he was always kind to me."

Then Elena walked up to them, and Sawyer hugged her. "Thank you all for coming," she said to the table, taking Sawyer's hand in hers. "Mateo speaks of you all with such respect and love."

"We think the world of your grandson," Curtis told her. "Matt, take care of them."

"Will do. I'll see you all on Monday."

•••••••••

"Mateo."

Matt looked up from his phone. Saturday morning, and he was planning on going back to his house after lunch. "Yes, Grandma?"

She beckoned at him, and he followed her into their bedroom. She stood by their closet. "I'm going to clean again this week. Is there anything in here you want?"

Matt stood still. He'd assumed that placing his grandfather's ashes into the ground the night before had been the hardest thing he'd ever done, but now, standing in front of their closet, he felt like he'd been kicked him in the stomach. "Um, yeah."

Reaching out, Matt picked up Hector's favorite cowboy boots and set them down on the bed. He took a couple of work shirts and a fancy guayabera shirt he'd worn on special occasions. An old straw hat that had seen better days and a big silver belt buckle. "What are you doing with the rest?"

When Matt turned around, he saw her crying. It was the first time she'd shed tears in front of him all week. Putting the hat and buckle down on the bed, Matt reached out and hugged her.

Elena wiped her eyes. "There's people out there who can wear these. No need for them to sit in here, not being used, making me sad. But it makes me happy, knowing some of his things will be with you for many years to come."

That night, he lay in bed and looked at the belt buckle he'd set on his nightstand. What if he kept it for fifty years? Would anybody want it? Would there be anyone in his life who would ask for it, cleaning out his possessions after he passed?

Unable to stop these thoughts, Matt rolled over and closed his eyes again, willing himself to fall asleep.

May

State assessment season was upon them, and the entire staff seemed to feel the pressure. Students took one cumulative exam at the end of the year, and despite being told the results didn't affect teacher raises or promotions, everyone felt that sense of dread that their students might not do well. Extra tutoring sessions, reviewing content from the beginning of the year that the students didn't remember, and more after school meetings. The teachers all seemed a little twitchier. Lunchroom conversations filled with worries and concerns about how their kids would perform.

"Gregg talked about trying Saturday tutoring sessions for Reading, but I think it's too late for that," Felipe said. "They know it, or they don't. We're not going to get much more in them."

"I've seen a sort of glassy look on their faces this morning." Alicia dragged her fork through her microwaved meal. "What about you, Matt? How are your kids looking?"

He shrugged. "My eighth-grade classes always worry me, and then they pull it out in the end. We'll see this year." Taking a bite of his sandwich, he added, "Me being gone a week didn't help."

"You couldn't help that." Kristine rested her hand on his arm. "Though I know Dorothy was a little worried, being gone so long in the beginning."

"Sawyer did a good job," Steve said. "They got a solid foundation."

"Still, she's going to worry—it's only natural." Alicia looked over at Matt as if they wanted to ask a question, but in the end the room fell silent, everyone eating quietly.

· · · · · · · · · ·

On the first day of testing, he saw Sawyer walking out of the front office, talking to Daisy. Taking a deep breath, he walked over to them. "Hey."

"Hi, Matt." Sawyer carried a bucket of supplies. "Looks like I'm helping with attendance."

On these special testing days, the school needed extra people to help on the campus. "I bet they're glad to get you." Matt heard his name being called. Turning his head, he saw Clint waving him down. "I'd better go, but…"

"Yeah," Sawyer answered. "I'll see you around."

Lunchtimes during testing usually provided some entertainment. Everyone's lunch schedule was different, so Matt walked into the lunchroom and saw a few unfamiliar faces, people he rarely ate with.

And of course, Sawyer had this lunch. He and Cora were settled on the far end of the table, deep in conversation when Matt walked in.

Fuck. The atmosphere of the room changed, and everyone quieted. *So much for avoiding office gossip.* "Got room for one more?" he asked, opening the fridge and taking out his insulated bag.

Keith Page waved him over, pointing at the empty seat next to him. Matt sat down and pulled out his sandwich.

Daisy walked in to get a drink from the soda machine, and made her way to Sawyer when she sighted him. "Hey, I saw you were at the coast in your last video. Did you have a good time?"

He nodded. "Oh yeah, the fishing was great. Different from where I'm from, but a lot of fun."

"Got any upcoming plans?" Stella asked, joining their discussion.

Sawyer bit his lip, obviously trying to avoid looking in Matt's direction. "I'm thinking about traveling east, maybe spend time in Louisiana and see if what I hear about New Orleans's cuisine is true. I imagine I might stay there a while."

Matt looked up, recalling that romantic trip for two he'd imagined for them, the one that had never materialized because…

Because of him.

"—and I heard the Carolinas have good barbecue."

A passionate debate began, people taking sides on the different types of sauce found in the various parts of the country. Matt looked down at this lunch, no longer hungry.

"You okay?" Keith asked.

"I'm good." Matt stood, gathering his trash. "I've just got a lot of stuff to do. Good luck, you guys." He left the room without looking back.

· · · • • • • • • · ·

"Ruiz."

Matt walked down the corridor toward the gym locker room and looked up.

Paul Cross waved at him. "Over here." He walked in that direction, following Paul past the gym and out of the school. "I need to get the soccer nets set up on the football field. Think you can help me with that?"

"Yeah, of course." It was a bright and sunny day, and the idea of spending the last hour of the day outdoors pleased him. "Feels good to hang out outside after being cooped up in the classroom testing all week."

"Tell me about it," Paul replied. They fell into an easy step together and soon made it to the football field. Paul pulled out his ring of keys and unlocked the chain-link gate to the field. "I wanted to talk to you too, and I thought we could do with some privacy."

Matt looked up, worried. Paul Cross was head coach at the school, and everyone knew that at any school in Texas, the head coach was one of the most powerful positions on campus. In some districts, they hired the head coach at new schools before the principal. "Yeah, of course. Anything wrong?" he asked, thinking this was bad news. Had all that shit preoccupied him too much this year? Was he not helping the staff or the kids enough? Maybe they didn't want him helping next year. "I screw something up?"

"No, nothing like that," Paul responded. "This isn't about work." They walked toward the athletic shed, a small portable building on one side of the field. Paul unlocked it and stepped inside. "How long have we known each other, Matt? Four years now? Five?" He carried out a bag of netting, handing it to Matt.

Matt wrinkled his brow, confused. "Ever since I got here." Paul grabbed the soccer goal frames, and they strolled out toward the football field. "Five years, yeah."

Paul cleared his throat as they approached the field. "Look, I'm not usually one to intrude in anyone's personal life, but I wanted to talk to you about what transpired earlier this year."

Matt froze. Was this about what had happened back in February, when that video had circulated the community? He felt like that chatter had just about died down, and now Paul was bringing it back up. "You know, I'm sorry about that. I didn't mean to embarrass anyone, or the team, or the school."

"This is what I'm saying. You didn't embarrass the school. You got caught kissing someone. Hell, I do that, and if a kid tapes it, I'm gonna get teased too. These kids and their cameras. We should take them all away. But I don't think you should let something like that make you change your mind about a relationship. It doesn't matter what other people think or say." He began putting a frame together, holding it steady as Matt secured the net onto it.

Matt waited until he'd finished before speaking. "It's not the same for you."

"You know, they weren't making fun of you for being gay." Paul sighed, shaking his head. "You're young, you're popular, your boyfriend is cute. Those kids didn't mean any harm."

"That's not exactly how it felt."

Paul glared at him, reaching for another frame, repeating the process. "I thought your skin was a little thicker than that. How can you let what other people think mess with you like that? I won't pretend like I understand what it is two guys see in each other, but I know someone in love, and it's clear you love that guy. So...just get your head out of your ass and stop letting what people think dictate your life."

Matt stopped, looking up from his task. "Sometimes what other people think matters."

"That's horseshit. I don't know many people who work harder than you, Matt, and all I can say is none of that is worth a damn if you're not happy. It's not much fun watching you mope around like some dog that's been kicked around." They finished the second net. "So, ask yourself—are you happy right now? 'Cause if you are, I'll shut up over here and we can set these up in silence."

Matt didn't speak, not until they'd finished the third goal. "I always thought you were a hard ass, Paul. When did you get so soft?" he asked, a hint of a smile on his face. He really had good friends.

Paul narrowed his eyes. "You son of a..." They both laughed, looking up to see all the athletes, girls and boys, running toward them, ready to play. "C'mon, Ruiz. Let's get these kids ready for high school."

·· ● ● ●· ● ● ·· ·

There is a point sometime each May where the end is not only in sight but also palpable. Teachers get that second wind, and conversations turned to job assignments for next year, who would leave, who'd move rooms, and what other changes would be happening.

With the end of the year approaching, Matt had his own final exams and presentations for his graduate program to work on when he got home from work. He'd taken to eating lunch at his desk to stay caught up on grading, but they were celebrating Steve's birthday on Friday, and they'd requested his presence in the lunchroom to help celebrate.

Alicia cut generous slices from a chocolate swiss roll. "Did you have plans for your birthday?" she asked Steve.

"Well, my birthday is actually Sunday, so Beth and I were thinking about taking Monday off and driving to the coast this weekend. I was calling around for a sub this morning, but no takers."

A few people glanced over at Matt, who ignored their stares.

Kristine groaned. "Good luck finding someone good. No one wants to come in because the kids all have summer fever."

"Sawyer's not available?" Matt asked, tired of the elephant in the room. "I haven't seen him in a while." He looked around the table. "No one is calling him for a job?" When no one said anything, Matt took a breath, drumming his fingers on the table. "Look, I appreciate what you're doing, but you all shouldn't stop using him because it didn't work out for us. That's not cool. He's a good guy and a great sub. Don't punish him because I'm an asshole incapable of a lasting relationship."

Silence. Matt realized now *he* was the teacher over-sharing embarrassing details.

Kristine broke the silence. "I don't think he's been taking jobs from this school. I guess it's...awkward for you guys." A couple of teachers looked at each other, then back at him. "Matt, are you okay?"

Matt put his fork down and sighed. Was Sawyer turning down jobs to spare Matt the embarrassment of being in the same building as him? Looking up, he caught Steve's eye and saw understanding there. Kristine too.

She understood. They all understood.

That was what Cora and Sabrina and Curtis and Paul had struggled to tell him. There wasn't any need to feel ashamed by what he felt for Sawyer. It was more embarrassing trying to hide it.

"Yeah, I'm alright. Thanks for asking." He stood, wiping his mouth on the brightly colored napkin. "Happy birthday, Steve." He stepped around and gave Steve a one-armed hug. "And thanks for dragging me out of my room for lunch today."

Alicia reached out and touched his arm. "We miss seeing your face. Don't be a stranger."

••••••••••

Matt blinked.

Reaching over, he touched his phone, turning off the alarm. 5:40 AM. He'd forgotten today was Memorial Day, and his alarm had gone off like it always did on weekdays. No gym, since he was at the ranch. He could go running outside; Pancho and Lefty would like it (well, Pancho would—Lefty was getting lazy in her old age). What else? Check if final grades had posted for the classes. Register for summer classes. Help Sabrina with the chores. Water the garden.

And it hit him. What was he doing all of this for? Who was he doing all of this for?

Worse, he'd hurt someone dear to him, a kind man who hadn't deserved Matt's anger.

He heard his grandfather's voice, urging him on. "*Come on, mijo. You did wrong. Now fix it.*"

Matt knew where to start.

Matt was in the kitchen when his grandmother walked in. "You're up early." She walked over and kissed his cheek on her way to the coffee pot. "Are you hungry?"

"Not really." He was looking through one of her cookbooks. When she glanced over at him, he smiled, the first smile he'd felt in weeks. Maybe months. "But I do have a favor to ask."

••••••••••

Matt: *Are you home? Can we talk?*

Matt sat, holding his phone in his hand waiting for the response he hoped for. A minute later, he got it.

Sawyer: *I'm home. Come on over.*

· · · · **·** **·** · · · ·

He knocked on Sawyer's door, carrying a small cake pan covered in foil. Rocking on his heels, he waited, but when no one answered, he guessed that maybe he'd gotten the message wrong. Raising his hand to knock again, he heard steps, the latch to the door being opened from the inside, and soon the door opened. "Sorry." Sawyer stepped back and held the door open. "Guess I drifted off." Looking down at the cake pan, he gave Matt a sad smile. "Come on in."

"Thanks." Matt stepped into the RV, setting the cake pan on the table near the door. "Hey, girl," he said as Biscuit trotted over, nudging his hand with her head. "Long time, no see." Looking back up at Sawyer, he exhaled. "How are you doing?"

"Good. Looks like the school year's wrapping up, so I'm making my summer plans, thinking about what I want to do next." He walked over to the sofa area, showing with his hand that Matt should sit.

"You're leaving for good then?" Matt asked, heart thumping fast in his chest.

"I guess. I mean, that was always the plan." Sawyer shrugged, looking down. "Don't think I expected to stay here this long, to be honest."

"But you did."

"Yeah." Matt caught Sawyer's eye and held that look. "How's Elena? Your sister too—is your family doing okay?"

Matt nodded. "Getting through it. Sad, but...I don't know. My grandparents had a good life, and my grandma says she's at peace with it all. I don't think she's in a hurry to join Grandpa soon, but she knows she'll see him again. It comforts her."

Sawyer sighed. "And how are you doing?"

"I miss him a lot," Matt said. "I mean, we almost lost my grandma ten years ago, but I guess we'd prepared ourselves for that if it happened. But this..." He gave him a sad smile. "I was not ready to say goodbye to him." Sawyer reached out and took his hand, and Matt laced their fingers together. "Don't leave me too," Matt whispered.

"Matt." Sawyer reached over and put his arms around him, pulling him close. "You're going to be fine."

But Matt shook his head. "I need you."

"Matt."

"I mean it. I'm so sorry, Sawyer, for all those things I said." He looked up at him. "I was such an ass to you, and I don't deserve any of your forgiveness, I know that. But all those plans I have mean nothing if you aren't standing next to me." Reaching for one of Sawyer's hands, he pulled it to his lips. "Right next to me."

Sawyer didn't look convinced...but he didn't push Matt away. "What do you want, Matt?" he asked tiredly.

What did he want? "I want a reason to be working so hard, someone at home who's proud of me. Someone I can come home to each night and talk about my day, the good and the bad. Someone who wants to tell me all about their day, the good and the bad. I want a partner." Matt cupped Sawyer's face in his hands, feeling that rough stubble on his fingertips. "You and me. I think we could be amazing together." Matt leaned in and kissed him, the softest brushing of lips against each other.

Again, Sawyer didn't push him away, but that wary look on his face was like a knife in Matt's heart, knowing he was responsible. "What about your plans?" Sawyer asked, still looking down.

"Same plans. Just realized they weren't complete." He stroked Sawyer's cheek. "Turns out, you were part of the plan, after all. The most important part." There was another long pause, and Matt felt his heart beating loud in his chest. "Tell me what I need to do to make things right."

Sawyer didn't answer. He glanced down at the pan on Matt's lap. "Is that what I think it is?"

"Yeah." Matt glanced down at the cake, then back up at Sawyer. "I'm told that this cake is guaranteed to make you love me again."

Now Sawyer smiled, a small one but a step in the right direction. Kissing Matt's forehead, he stood and reached into a drawer, pulling out a fork. He waved it at Matt and returned to the sofa. "Guess it's time to find out," he said, pulling off the foil and taking a bite.

Matt lay on his side, staring out the window next to Sawyer's bed. The sun was going down, and he could see cars driving off in the distance. Sawyer emerged from the bathroom and slid behind him, those long arms wrapping around his torso. Matt reached for one of Sawyer's hands, lacing their fingers together. He remembered another time they were like this, another apology, another reconciliation.

Uncertainty still lingered in the air, and despite their current nakedness, Matt was still afraid to speak. Afraid to hear it hadn't been enough to win Sawyer back. But Matt's eyes closed when he felt those soft lips press against the back of his neck. "I'm sorry, babe. For everything."

"I know." Sawyer's breath was warm against Matt's skin.

"What can I do to make it up to you?"

"It's not like that. Matt..." There was that hesitation in Sawyer's voice again. "Don't you worry we might be too different?"

"No." He shifted, turning around until they lay face to face. "I love that difference. Fuck, I think I need it. When I'm with you, I see so much more than my spreadsheet. I see what life is all about, the beauty and the sadness, and I'd miss all of it if you weren't with me."

Sawyer's thumb rubbed along Matt's jaw, a small smile on his face at Matt's words. "I was with this other guy once. The only other serious relationship I've had, and it hurt like hell when it ended. But the lesson I took away from that experience was that I was worth being someone's priority. I'm not asking to be your whole life, Matt, but I deserve to be important. I know it looks like I don't have my shit together, but I want a partner in this great big adventure that we're on. I want—"

Matt wanted to roll on top of this man, take him inside him again, and show Sawyer just how important he was to Matt. But the sex was so easy. It was Matt's actions outside of this bed that Sawyer needed. "Will you take me somewhere this summer? We can go on a trip, anywhere you want to go. You can show me what you love to do. I want to see it." He leaned in for another soft kiss. "I want to help you."

Sawyer's eyes caught Matt's. "You want to go on a road trip with me?"

"You and the girl, yeah." As if on cue, Biscuit jumped off her dog bed on the far side of the RV and scrambled toward them. Matt reached over and scooped her up, setting her next to them. "What do you say? I love you, Sawyer. Will you give us a chance?"

Now it was Sawyer's turn to reach out, pulling Matt toward him. One kiss melted into another. "*Querido*," Sawyer murmured, his eyes dancing when Matt smiled back at him. "Did I say that right?"

Matt nodded, answering with a searing kiss of his own.

June

To: All_Staff_HaysMS

From: Curtis White

Date: June 4

Subject: Last day of school faculty meeting agenda

We made it through another year, Hawks. Please plan to meet bright and early Friday, June 8 at 9 AM in the cafeteria. PTA is providing donuts and coffee. Admin will be in their offices all day to sign off on textbooks, classroom keys, and technology returns. Any staff not returning next year must complete an exit interview with me before they leave today...

·· • • • • • • ··

M att stood in front of his room, looking around in wonder, thinking back at the year—and what a year it'd been. He'd walked into this room back in August, angry they had given him a time-sucking babysitting task, the last thing he needed before embarking on an already jam-packed school year. He couldn't help but laugh thinking about it now; what a bitter little man he'd been.

And now?

Matt stacked his textbooks in neat rows, waiting for his turn to take them to the textbook closet. He had unplugged his computer and printer. He looked at his empty walls, the posters and math charts locked in his closet with his paper trays and other supplies. They'd wait all summer for him, until he came back next year, and the cycle began again.

The idea made him smile.

Glancing down at his phone, he noted the time. Twenty minutes to eight, still a little time before he had to be in the cafeteria for the meeting, but he knew people would be there already. The tired staff somehow found that spark of energy, the idea of ten weeks off so close they could taste it.

He looked around the room one more time. It had been quite the year, but it was over. There was nothing more to do, so he grabbed his backpack and jogged downstairs toward the cafeteria for the last time this year.

· · · · ● ● · ● · · · ·

"And we're going to be saying goodbye to Eva Moody. Eva has taken a position as head librarian at the high school, so our loss is their gain. Eva, we will miss you and your bright smile, but we all wish you the best of luck."

Eva stood, a sad look on her face as she waved at everyone. She clasped her hands together when the staff clapped and wished her well.

"Finally, please be sure to give your summer contact information to Rosa…"

"Hey, you." Cora sidled up next to Matt during their break, one arm snaking around his waist as she hugged him. "We made it."

"We did," he repeated, hugging her back. "Though there were a few days I wasn't sure that would happen."

"But you did, despite it all. And in the end, things turned out good here, right?" She touched his shoulder. "How's your boyfriend?"

It still felt so strange to think of Sawyer like that. "He's great." Matt couldn't contain his grin. "He's working on a new video today and when I get out of here, we're going to the ranch for a few days to help out before we leave."

Her eyes widened. "That's right! Where are you going?"

"Big Bend National Park, for starters, before it gets too hot. Then maybe into New Mexico." It frightened him how nonchalant Sawyer was as he prepared for this trip, just driving the Airstream west and seeing what looked interesting during the two weeks between school ending and his summer classes starting. "All I know is we're taking turns driving that monster of an RV, so that's also terrifying."

"At least you don't have to worry about hotels." She laughed. "It'll be fine, and you know it. You look happy, Matt. I hope you guys have a glorious summer. You deserve it, more than anyone I know."

· · · · ●· ● · · · ·

Matt walked into the front office to turn in his classroom keys. He sat next to Paul at the end of the line of anxious teachers, all ready to leave. "Waiting for Rebecca?"

Paul nodded. "I've got to hand in my keys and then turn around and check them out again so I can come back this summer and condition the field. Asinine." He shook his head. "You got any plans coming up?" Matt told him about the trip he and Sawyer had planned. Paul's genuine smile and interest in the trip touched Matt more than he'd expected. "Not going to lie, Ruiz, I'm jealous as fuck of you guys traveling in that Airstream. Always wanted to do that, drive an RV around and camp wherever."

"It should be fun. And you?" They watched as the door to Rebecca's office opened, Felipe exiting and Stella entering.

"Letty's family is from Boston, so I think we're flying up there for the Fourth of July. Her little sister had a baby a couple months ago…" They talked for a few more minutes, and then the door opened, and it was Paul's turn. "Hey, if I don't see you before you head out, have a great summer." They shook hands, and Paul went inside the office, closing the door behind him.

A few more people walked by, and pleasantries were exchanged. Nurse Norma and her family were traveling to Disney World. Laverne was starting a patio project, redoing her deck herself. Dan's son was going to be a freshman at Texas Tech, and the family would go up to move him into an apartment. Soon, the door opened. Paul gave him a salute as he exited, and Matt walked inside.

"Mr. Ruiz." Rebecca had a small silver locked box on her cluttered desk, covered in small clear bags filled with keys. "How is your family doing?" she asked, giving him a sympathetic look.

"Everyone's good. We miss my granddad, but in a way, he's still around us, wherever we look."

"I can imagine, especially out there on your land."

Matt handed her the keys to his classroom and the gym.

"We'll see you back next year, right?"

"That's the plan," he answered. "It's strange, isn't it? Leaving here for ten weeks, and then everyone comes back in the fall and we all just sort of pick right up where we left off, as if we were gone for the weekend."

"I think about that too." Rebecca noted his name and had him sign off that he'd returned the keys. "You have a splendid summer, Matt."

"You too." Matt stood and made his way out of the office and down the hallway. He was done.

> Matt: *How are things going?*
>
> Sawyer: *Great. Another hour and I'll be done. The kitchen's a disaster area. I'll need to clean up before we leave.*

"Hey, Matt." Looking up, he spotted April, carrying a plant and walking toward the front door. "Some of us are going to Gringo's for lunch. Going away party for Eva." Teachers could leave once they locked their classrooms up and checked their classroom keys in. "You wanna join us?"

He pulled out his phone and grinned. "Yeah, that sounds good. I'll meet you all there."

> Matt: *Heading to Gringo's with the gang. Think you can join us? I'll help you clean up when we're done.*
>
> Sawyer: *Sounds so good. I'll meet you there. Order me a margarita if you get there before I do.*

Matt pocketed his phone. Looking back down the hallway, he remembered about all that had happened this year. Good things, bad things, and yet Matt knew it was a year he'd never forget. Turning back toward the front doors, he pushed them open and jogged down the steps toward his truck.

It was going to be an amazing summer.

Thank you!

O nce again, thank you for reading this book. Want to find out what happens next? Head to Argentina's website (argentinaryder.com) and pre-order the next book in the *Rio Riendo* series. You can also pick up a couple of free stories set in the *Rio Riendo* universe.

For a debut novel such as this, reviews are critical to its success so please, if you feel inclined, share your thoughts and reactions on any of the major platforms.

About Argentina

Argentina Ryder spent her early career as a high school teacher in Texas, sharing her love of geography and traveling with her students. After completing her Masters in Education, she worked as a Curriculum and Instruction consultant while working on her first novel.

Argentina's bucket list includes visiting all the national parks and running a ten-minute mile. She spends free time in her garden, kayaking Texas rivers, and littering her house with various DIY projects. Her red slider, Pebbles, enjoys frozen strawberries, basking under her UV light, and spending quality time outside on sunny days while Lucrezia, her Siamese, mostly just sleeps.

She lives with her family and her pets, and is currently working on the next book in her *Life, Love, and Other Inequalities* series. You can sign up for her newsletter at her website (argentinaryder.com) to keep up with what's going on in her world and get sneak peaks at what's coming up.

•••••••••

Facebook - @Argentina-Ryder-Books
Twitter - @books_ryder
Instagram - @argentina_ryder_books

www.ingramcontent.com/pod-product-compliance
Lightning Source LLC
Chambersburg PA
CBHW050145110726
47898CB00008B/2678